Seasons of Life

Seasons of Life

Sandra Engelbrecht

To order additional copies of this book, contact:
Xlibris Corporation
0-800-644-6988
www.xlibrispublishing.co.uk
Orders@Xlibrispublishing.co.uk
301139

"A special thanks to Lara Scholtz for the translation and to Maureen and Piet Uys for their moral support."-

Chapter 1

Abby Spence is looking at the big old grey building across the street. The big letters that is written in red on the building proves that she is at the right place.

Blake Attorneys. The interview is at ten o'clock and on the sixth storey. Lost in thoughts she starts counting the storeys of the big old building. "As luck would have it." Abby mumbles sarcastically to herself. "The big building only has six storeys, witch means that my interview is right at the top storey."

Suddenly it feels like she is loosing her nerve. Since Abby's childhood she managed to develop some fears, such as acrophobia and arachnophobia.

Abby looks down at her wrist watch to see what the time is, it's twenty to ten.

This morning when she looked at herself in the mirror, the dark circles beneath her eyes, were a testimony of the sleepless night she had, had. She just hopes nobody suspect a thing. The last thing she needs now is someone noticing that she looks like she had just risen from the dead. It's been going on for quite a while now.

The reason why Abby is dog-tired this morning, is because of little Jimmy. Last night he was constantly complaining about a sore throat, and he seems to be very feverish.

He woke her up through the night and Abby went to sit on the edge of the little boy's bed. She bent over him and rubbed her lips against his forehead to try to determine if he had a fever. When her lips touched his forehead there was no doubt about the fever. She went to the bathroom to get a wet cloth. Back in the room she sponged him until the fever subsided. She then tucked him in again and went to sleep. In less than no time, Jimmy called her again, and the scene occurred for the second time that night.

This morning Abby took the little boy to the elderly woman that lives in the apartment next door. Aunt Ella has been looking after Jimmy during the day while Abby's at work. Aunt Ella is the motherly type. Although she is in her early sixty's, she still lives life to the fullest. Abby has never heard her complain about anything and it amazes her. The road chosen for her was sometimes bumpy and had many crossroads telling by the lines on her face it shows that she didn't always choose the right one. Yet her eyes portray a certain softness something that makes you feel that you can confide in her. Despite the fact Abby still can't seem to bring her to talk to Aunt Ella about the crossroad that she is standing before now.

With a smile on Abby's face, she thinks about Aunt Ella. The conversation which they had before she left for her interview.

"Morning dear." Aunt Ella greeted her with a friendly smile. "Morning Aunt Ella." Abby walked past her, with the sleeping boy in her arms straight to the only bedroom in the apartment. She laid him down very carefully on the bed, and made sure he was comfortable before she walked out the room and closed the door behind her.

Abby noticed aunt Ella was looking at her in a strange way, but Abby didn't bat an eyelid. Then suddenly the Aunt Ella asked: "What's eating you dear?" Abby sighed and answered her: "I'm dog-tired, neither Jimmy nor myself got any sleep last night."

"Was it one of those nights?"

"I'm afraid so, and it's been happening more often. I just can't seem to understand why? The last time I took Jimmy to the doctor, he prescribed an antibiotic for Tonsillitis. What I can't understand, is why there is no sign of improvement? He isn't getting better, in fact he is getting worse." Aunt Ella walked towards Abby and placed her hand on the young woman's shoulder and said: "My dear, don't despair. Have faith, because there is a God that heals. All you've got to do is fully trust in Him and pray for Jimmy."

Trusting God is like a blind alley. She had been down that road before. How can she put her trust in God when He is the one who took away her family? He took them away without consideration for me. Unaware of the tears rolling down her cheeks, the night of the accident appears in her head. The pain, sorrow, heartache and loneliness fill her like so many times before. She was so excited when she got the news that her family was coming to visit.

When the doorbell rang, she couldn't control her excitement.

She rushed to the front door and opened it. The people standing there were not her family, but two police officer's. If Abby had known back then what she knew now, she would never have opened the door. If she could've prevented anything from happening that night, she would've.

As much as she tried to forget what happened, the memories are still unblemished in her mind. The police officers informed her about the tragic news. Her family died in a car accident. This was too much to bear, and she wouldn't acknowledge it. It was a bitter pill she refused to swallow. She was quarrelling with them, until she fell to the floor in devastation. The last memory she recalled, was the doctor giving her an injection, and she fell asleep.

Her parents, Molly Spence and Joe Spence were amorous people. Although they were not wealthy, the love they had for one another and their children, enriched their lives and amount to all the other shortcomings.

Molly taught their daughters everything about love, honesty and trust. Joe on the other hand nurtured their faith and taught them how to pray.

Although the sisters were identical twins, they were as poles apart in temperament. Abby is the quite and responsible one, while Cathy was an eager beaver. She was the type of person who would always burn her bridges. One day Cathy entered the kitchen while Molly was preparing supper, and she looked like she had seen a ghost.

Molly noticed it, and was very concerned about her daughter. She walked up to Cathy and took her hand into her own and with great distress in her eyes she asked: "What's wrong my darling? You looked like you've seen a ghost." Cathy looked up in her mothers eyes, and began crying when she answered her: "Oh mother, I . . . . I'm . . . . Pregnant." From the expression on Molly's face, her daughter could tell she was devastated.

Cathy holds her breath, while waiting for her mother to go bananas. Yet to her surprise, nothing happened. Molly just looked at Cathy with despair in her eyes. Later that night Molly spilled the beans about Cathy's pregnancy, Joe felt like words failed him. After a while he looked at his daughter Cathy and asked: "Who is the man responsible? Cathy just shook her head. She was unable to say anything. The only thing Joe said before he stood up and left the kitchen was "blood is thicker than water".

Until today nobody knows who Jimmy's father is.

A loud noise from behind brings Abby back to reality, she then realizes she had been day dreaming. "Oh come on Abby, pull yourself together." She wipes her tears and opens her bag to find a little pocket mirror, to make sure all the traces of tears are gone.

She straightens her outfit and begins to cross the busy road towards the big old grey building. She finds herself standing in front of two glass doors and takes a deep breath, to clam herself. She closes her eyes for a moment and mumbles to herself: "Abby you know how important it is for you to get this job, so just relax and give it all you've got." Abby gathers her emotions, opens her eyes and enters the building. Once she is inside she is inundated with all the activity taking place around her.

Suddenly she is overwhelmed that she has an urge to run for the hills. Just as she is about to answer her urge she hears the voice of a woman beside her, she turns around only to find and elderly lady dressed in a black designer suit, with a friendly yet professional smile on her face. Abby can see she is well groomed with long brown hair curled into a French role. Abby wonders were the lady came from; it was as if she appeared out of thin air. The elderly lady then says: "Good morning Ms, how can I be of assistance?"

"Good . . . . morning . . . . Ms, I am here . . . . F . . . . for an interview."

"What is your name?"

"My name is Abby . . . . Abby Spence."

The elderly lady walks toward the large antique reception desk and picks up a clip board. While the elderly lady is standing at the desk. Abby looks at her and thinks to herself, they have chosen the perfect candidate to be the face of the company. The elderly lady pages through the contents on the clip board and returns to Abby.

"Ms Spence, which position are you applying for?"

"I am applying for the junior typist position."

The elderly lady looks at the clip board again dragging her red painted finger nail through the pages, her nail comes to a Holt, and she looks up at Abby and says: "Please follow me."

Abby follows the lady towards the elevator. While waiting for it to reach the ground floor, Abby turns to admire the reception area with its spacious Victorian style. Although the room is filled with warm colours and strong lighting, she can't help but feel a chill down her spine. Here and there she sees Victorian portraits. At the main entrance with the glass doors, she sees pot plants with palm trees thriving in pride on either side.

The tiles on the floor is with intertwined colours, along with the furniture and decor appears to be antique. The sound of the bell from the elevator puts her admiration to an end. Seconds later they are in the elevator on the way to the 6th floor, in complete silence. The lift stops and the doors open, Abby follows the elderly lady down the long corridor with bare white walls. They reach a door at the end of the corridor.

The elderly lady opens the door and leads the way into an office. She turns to Abby and says: "Have a seat; I will be with you in a moment." The elderly lady then walks toward another door which leads into a second office.

Cal Blake sits with his head in his hands, since the interviews are not going as well as he expected. Not one of the candidates is fully qualified for the position. He has been busy with interviews since 7 o' clock this morning. He wanted to start early as he had a very important meeting with one of the company's financial managers.

For a moment he thinks about his previous typist, Kate Freeman. She was very professional. Not only did she do her job flawlessly, she could also make the best Coffee. She was never late for work and she never stayed away from the office.

One morning Kate walked into Cal's office placing a folded letter on his desk, without saying a word she turned and walked out of the office. He was so busy he didn't take note of the folded letter; she had placed on his desk.

Only later that day while packing up to go home did him notice it. As he read it his blood ran cold only to discover that she had resigned giving one months notice because she is getting married. However, she had so much leave accumulated she would not be returning to work out her notice period. He thought to himself, I'm now stuck between the devil and the deep sea. He grabbed his phone and tried to contact her to see if he could convince her to change her mind, but the attempt was unsuccessful. He then realised he would have to replace her immediately; he thought to himself, what I need now is an angel of mercy!

A knock at the door brings Cal back from his train of thought "Come in!" he answered with a petulant voice. The elderly lady enters his office and says: "Cal, Ms Spence is here for her interview, can I send her in?"

"Yes Irene you can send her in."

"I'll do so." She leaves the office to inform Ms Spence that Mr Blake is ready to meet with her. "Ms Spence, Mr Blake will see you now."

Abby nods her head and walks through the door which Irene held open for her.

The office is big, with a soft cream colour on the walls that reflects warmth. Abby's mouth hung wide open about the space of the room. She thinks to herself, my whole apartment could fit into this room without a doubt. Here and there are framed certificates against the walls. She noticed that the tiles are very similar to the ones in the reception area. Right in the centre there is a large desk with two leather chairs in front of it.

She sees a man behind the desk with his head hanging; it looks like he is reading something. Abby, not sure of what to do, decides to hold her position. Cal then realises he has company and lifts his head. What he sees in front of him looks like a school girl who lost her bearings. Two bright green eyes are staring at him. Cal stands up and walks towards her. He stands dead still in front of her, with his hands on his sides and greets her: "Good morning Ms Spence" he extends his hand toward her.

Abby practically needs to bend over backwards to look him in the eyes. WOW, she thinks to herself, not only is he very tall, but he's also easy on the eye. She takes his hand and it feels like she has been hit by lightning. She gazes at his hands, big beautiful bronzed hands with strong straight fingers. She wonders how it would feel if those hands embraced her whole body. Abby, ashamed of her thought mumbles: "Good morning Sir."

She pulls back her hand, and before she can stop herself, she continues to gaze at him. The designer shirt he is wearing pulls tightly across his chest. She thinks she can see his biceps though the material. His stomach is flat and no sign of any unwanted body fat.

She is certain he must be spending a lot of time in the gym. His legs look as though they could be well sculpted. She gazes at his face, he has a firm mouth and his jaw line is shaped perfectly. His black hair is short on his head. Cal's voice brings her back from her lustful train of thought, when he asked: "If I have your approval of me, can we start the interview Ms Spence?"

Abby suddenly realises what she did, and takes one step back. A feeling of embarrassment overcomes her and she begins to blush.

With amusement in his eyes he looks at the women. He tries to recall the last time he saw a women blush like that. The women he is used to never blush when they undress him with their eyes.

The little school girl standing in front of him is pure and innocent. Her bushy black hair, tied back in the scuff of her neck begging him to free them. He puts his hands in his trouser pockets to prevent temptation getting the better of him. Her skin is the colour of a peach rose and her mouth is slightly open begging to be kissed.

Her beauty is phenomenal. Cal takes a deep breath and says: "Have a seat Ms Spence." He shows her to the desk and pulls out a chair; she anxiously grabs the invitation with both hands. Cal scurries around his desk looking for her curriculum Vitae. "Here we are" he says.

He studies her CV thoroughly in silence. It's so quite you can hear a pin drop. After a while (which feels like an eternity to Abby) he looks her straight in the eye and asks her a question: "Ms Spence, I see on your CV that you are currently working at a restaurant, as an admin clerk. Have you ever worked in an office environment?"

"No."

"How long have you been residing in Bloemfontein?"

"Approximately two years"

Cal continues studying the CV.

Abby feels a tingle on her leg and drops her hand to wipe the feeling away, only to find something hairy under her hand. Abby knows she shaved her legs the night before, so it can't be her leg hairs that she is feeling. Oh my gosh it's moving and is on top of her hand, she looks down to see what it is and her blood runs cold. Her entire body goes lame, her throat tightens and she can't get a word out. Cal lifts his head to say something and looks into a pale face with eyes as wide as saucers.

He wonders what's wrong with her, is she maybe having some sort of attack? Her eyes haven't rolled towards the back of her head yet, so he is sure that she will be just fine. Maybe she is just nervous. On the other side of the desk Abby feels like she is about to die.

She sits dead still not moving a muscle or batting an eyelid. The spider feels to her bigger than her hand. She can't bring herself to look nor can she bear the thought of the spider on her hand.

Everything inside her is shouting for the spider to go away but he wouldn't budge. Cal sees the change in her eyes from as wide as saucers to fear. What in the world could it be that she is afraid of? It can't be me. He decides the only way he will know is to ask her: "Is something bothering you Ms Spence?"

Abby opens her mouth in the attempt to say something but nothing comes out, all she can do is nod her head. Cal sees her nodding and he walks around the desk to her. He sits on the other leather chair and looks at her.

Cal opens his mouth to say something and he noticed a movement on her leg, he bends down to have a look and sees something familiar. His facial expression is a testimony of great relief. "Flippy" she hears him say and he removes the spider from her hand. Abby is extremely relieved and it feels as though she could kiss him because he saved her from a near death experience, but then she remembered what he said when he took the spider off her hand.

She is not sure if she was hallucinating but she is almost certain that she heard him call the spider Flippy. No, no she must be wrong it just can't be who in their right mind would ever give such a thing a name. No she must be confused but then she hears him say again: "Flippy, where were you been all this time, I searched everywhere for you."

"What?" Abby screeched, "are you talking to a spider, did I hear you correctly does the spider have a name?" She asks with confusion. "How could you talk to a spider, an ugly hairy long eight legged creature?" Before Abby thinks of any further ferocious things to say describing the creature, Cal interrupts her: "Ms this is Flippy and he is part of my collection." Abby replies almost chocking on her words: "You're what?" "Yes you heard me correctly he is one of my collections, him and his family." She asks him in disgust: "I can't believe what you just said, is their more?" Without saying a word he disappears into a secret door in the wall. All the occurrences of the day were flashing repeatedly through her mind.

She can make sense of everything except, the family of spiders. Cal enters the office again: "I am extremely sorry about what happened earlier, everything is under control, we can continue." He takes his seat in the chair behind the desk and is ready to proceed. Abby knows that she will never be able to share an environment with those creatures. It doesn't matter to her whether they are locked away or not, just the thought of it made her want to leave like a bat out of hell.

In a flat spin she gets up out of her chair, grabbing her handbag and storms toward the door.

In a hurry she falls over her own feet only to find herself feeling like she has egg on her face. Cal who saw the whole thing happens and is now on his feet. He rushes over to her where she is still lying on the floor, he reaches out to extend a helping hand but she refuses to accept it. Impatiently she says: "Don't bother, I don't need your help!" He steps back not understanding why she is so abrupt.

She tries to lift herself from the floor when suddenly she feels a sharp pain shooting through her foot. Just as she is about to fall for the second time, she feels two strong hands breaking her fall. Cal with an iron grip keeps her upright with her back towards him.

Abby looks down at his strong hands wrapped around her middle and feels her legs wanting to give way. The fact that he is holding her so tightly wakes up a feeling inside her that she has never experienced before.

It's an amazing yet dangerous feeling at the same time. To her despair she realises she needs to get away from him as soon as possible because of these feelings. She had embarrassed herself enough for one day and wants to pull away from him but she feels his grip is solid and her attempt fails. He feels her attempt and says: "Calm down Ms, have a seat, we first have to determine how badly you are injured." A frustrated Abby let him have his way. He makes sure that she is comfortable before bending down to have a look at her injury. Cal lifts her sore foot and quickly removes the black shoe.

Abby is relived that she is sitting; if she hadn't been she would have fainted from his sensational touch running up her leg. Cal notices her leg is shaking and accepts it as part of the shock. He turns his attention towards the shoe, the hill that is as thin as a nail grabs his attention.

He looks up at her with amusement in his eyes and says: "I'm surprised you haven't broken your neck in these nails yet?" Abby looks at the shoe's hill and noticed for the first time how dangerous the hill really is. She wouldn't normally wear this kind of attire, but the only choice she had was Hobson's choice.

She couldn't take something from her own closet, nor did she have any money to buy something. Since she took Jimmy under her wing, she has been struggling to make ends meet. She leant the clothes from her best friend Sally. Then Abby looks at the shoe and thinks to herself, how long it took me to get used to these shoes . . . . To be honest with myself I don't think I am, but nobody needs to know.

Abby looks up at Cal and blushes again. He sees that she is blushing and decides to use it to his advantage, he brings the attention back to the shoe with a devilish look in his eyes trying to keep a straight face and asks: "Is this the latest fashion or are you trying to impress someone?" Abby is infuriated by his question. Her green eyes, a mixture of anger and humiliation looked as if they could spit fire when she answered: "I'm not trying to impress anyone; I wear these shoes every day." In the back of her mind her guilty conscious is telling her she is lying, but she brushes it off as a necessary little white lie.

She wanted to make a good first impressing and that is why she borrowed the clothes. She sees a smile on his face and she can't seem to look away, not even for a second. He is a site for sore eyes but with that smile, he could make a nun forget her vows.

Cal notices the effect that his mouth has on Abby and can't resist but to kiss her. He stares at her with his brown eyes intertwined with hers. Before Abby could find herself he leans in to kiss her. The sweet taste of her lips makes him long for more, he then caresses her.

This is her first kiss and it was done with utmost passion and emotion. Emotions neither of them had ever experienced. They forget about everything around them. The only thing in existence is the two of them here and now. Of all the women he has kissed before none of them could compare or even come close to the passion she awoke in him.

All of a sudden she pulls back with a pale face and tears in her eyes, he looks at her with amazement in his eyes and thinks to himself, is it possible that the kiss means so much it would bring her to tears. He says to Abby: "I didn't realise a kiss would mean so much to you, that you would be so emotional about it." Abby replies under her breath: "I'm not crying because you kissed me . . . I am . . . . crying because . . . . you're standing on my injured foot and it hurts." He looks with complete embarrassment not sure what to do with himself. Abby says once again under her breath: "Would you please get . . . off . . . my foot."

Chapter 2

Aunt Ella and Jimmy are working in the garden on a warm summer's morning. Aunt Ella is digging holes to plant the Dahlia bulbs in the ground, while Jimmy fascinates himself by removing the weeds. While working they are having a chat about this and that. Jimmy points to the plants asking their names and Aunt Ella answers with enthusiasm.

She is very proud of her small garden and tries to spend as much time in it as her back would allow it. She fell down the stairs from the second floor while collecting the rent. As care taker it is one of her responsibilities. Luckily the injuries she sustained were not too serious. The doctor warned her although she didn't break anything she should still be very careful because of her age. At first Abby didn't like the idea of Jimmy staying with Aunt Ella because Jimmy could be quite a hand full. She couldn't expect Aunt Ella to scamper after Jimmy. Aunt Ella, politely told Abby: "You should not worry about that, I prefer the company of a young child because they are always so straight forward and honest, it can get very lonely sometime and Abby . . . . I'm not unhealthy." Together they laughed about Aunt Ella's remark and Abby stopped protesting. Aunt Ella plants her last bulb and glances up to see were Jimmy is. He is playing with his toy cars in the sand. As she watches him she thinks back on the past six months. He has changed a great deal since the day Abby introduces the brown eyed boy with light brown hair, he was very shy and a bit of an introvert to her. Although he is not like the other three year olds, she has seen before, he is spontaneous yet silent at times. Aunt Ella was amazed at how well he had adapted to his surroundings. She feels a certain sorrow for his situation as Abby has not yet explained to him what has happened to his family. Jimmy is aware of the accident because he was also in the car, what he is not aware of, is that he was the only survivor. Why the Lord saved his life, she will never know but she will always be grateful for it. Aunt Ella's thoughts turn to Abby. The poor child's life has been turned upside down since the accident. Not once did she hesitate to take Jimmy into her home, heart and life. Abby is in denial and sees Jimmy as hope that her family will someday return. The thing that bothers Aunt Ella the most is that Abby has not yet spoken about the death of her family and every time Aunt Ella tries to touch on the subject she closes up like a book and makes a bolt for it. In the past Abby was in church every Sunday but ever since the accident she seems to be coming up with excuses not to go. Aunt Ella closes her eyes and prays for Abby like so many times before. Lord, please help Abby see that your will isn't always something that we can understand. Even though she may not see it yet, you have a reason for everything. She cuts the prayer short when she feels a little hand on her arm. She looks down and sees Jimmy with a confused look on his face, he asks: "Why is your eyes close? Are you shleeping?" With a smile on her face she replies: "No my dear I'm not sleeping, I'm talking to Jesus." Jimmy looks at her inquisitively and asks: "What did you shay to him?" Trying to buy time not knowing how to explain what she was praying for she answers: "Jimmy, it's getting hot outside, I think it's time to go in." She takes his hand and they enter the house. In the kitchen she turns to him and asks: "What would you like to drink?"

"May I have some bunny miwk, pwease?" Aunt Ella laughs and says: "You go get us the milk and I'll make some for the both of us." Jimmy looks at Aunt Ella in amazement. "Does you awso drink bunny miwk? I fought it was only for chiwdren" Aunt Ella just laughs and says: "Who told you that? Did you know that bunny milk is my favourite drink?"

"Mine to. She tells him to have a seat while she makes it. Jimmy takes a seat with his legs crossed Indian style. He looks around the room; suddenly a little box on the coffee table grabs his attention. He jumps off the chair and walks over to the box. He picks it up and with a curios look in his eyes, he asks: "What is this?" Aunt Ella, turns around with the two drinks in hand and places them on the wooden table, she takes a seat on the wooden chair. She looks at him and says: "That is my memory box." Jimmy frowns and she can see that he doesn't understand. She continues to explain: "That is the box I put all of the reminders in of my loved ones. When I miss them, I look at the photos and remember the good times we had together and then I don't miss them as much." He walks towards her with the memory box in his hands: "May I wook at them, pwease?" He holds out the box. Aunt Ella takes it from him and opens it. He takes the open box and returns to his chair. He takes the contents of the box out carefully. The same person appears on all the photos. It's a little girl with an angel face and bright blue eyes. Her blonde hair curls up around her face. She smiles with her petite hands placed on her cheeks. Jimmy doesn't understand and asks: "Who is dis?" Aunt Ella takes the photo from Jimmy and stares at it. Her death was so sudden, one moment they were drinking cool drink in the cafe and the next there was a truck through the cafe window, in the place of where the little girl was sitting. She panicked and started looking for Mia, all she found was a puddle of blood with Mia curled up in a ball. She fell to her knees and held the deceased Mia in her arms. Suddenly the place was crawling with people offering to help. The heartache from that day returns to her heart along with all the questions she had. She remembers all the nights she quarrelled with the Lord. Mia was only 5 years old, why did she die so soon? For years they struggled to conceive a child and eventually when they did, it changed their whole lives. The doctor warned her to take it easy as she was 35 years old and there was a strong chance of her loosing the baby. The doctor had no reason for concern as the pregnancy went smoothly and the baby was born healthy. After the death of Mia her husband could not accept it. He tried drinking his sorrows away; when that didn't work he eventually took his own life. Aunt Ella was angry at God. How could he give her a child and take her away with the blink of an eye. How could he make such a coward of a man to take his own life and leave her alone with all the broken pieces of her heart to pick up? One thing that she forgot and didn't realise at the time was that she was never alone. Had she been alone she would never had been able to work through the tragedy. Suddenly she remembers that Jimmy is still there and he is waiting for an answer. She looks at him and answers with a hoarse voice: "Her name is Mia and she was my little girl." After thinking for a while Jimmy asks: "Aunt Ella, whe is she now?"

"God came and took her, my dear."

"Why did he take her? Whe did he take her?"

She takes a deep breath and reaches over the table holding his hand. She thinks to herself, what would a child his age know about death?

"Heaven Jimmy . . . . He took her to heaven"

Jimmy remembers that his gramps told him a lot about Jesus and heaven. His gramps told him heaven is beautiful and it's far up in the sky, but you can't get there in an aeroplane. "Is God goin to bwing hew back?"

Aunt Ella can't hold back her tears any longer; she takes the two empty glasses and turns away from him so that he can't see her tears. She places the glasses into the sink. Crying as she answers Jimmy: "One day . . . One day I'll see her again."

Chapter 3

Cal opens the passenger door of his luxury Mercedes for Abby and helps her in. He walks around the car to the driver's side and gets in. Abby reluctantly objects for the millionth time: "Mr Blake it's not necessary to take me home. I know you are a very busy man and I don't want to waste your time. You can drop me off at the bus stop; I'll be fine from there."

It doesn't look as if he is listening to her, because he isn't responding. The only thing he says is: "Fasten your seatbelt." He turns on the engine and drives towards the underground parking exit. All of a sudden Cal is being very abrupt and Abby can't understand why. As they reached the exit he asks: "Where do you live?" Abby mentions the name of the block of flats and the area which it is situated in. He looks at her with ridicule in his eyes.

He frowns and drives in the direction of a less fortunate suburb. They drive in silence. Abby stares out the window, not that she sees anything interesting. She just doesn't want to look at him. She bites her tongue trying not to attack him about his behaviour. She saw immediately in the look he gave her that he disapproved of the area she lives in.

A thought out of nowhere appears in her mind, would he have kissed me had he known where I come from? She blushes just thinking about the kiss. She pulls herself together and thinks, whether he likes where I live or not, that's his problem, not mine. Still it bothers her that he was so judgemental.

Cal, lost in his own thoughts, asks himself, how is it possible that the women sitting next me could end up an area like that? Her appearance says otherwise. When he broke her fall he happened to see the label of her attire and it was not the type of clothing that someone from that type of area would be able to afford. Something doesn't make sense.

He was seldom wrong when it came to reading people. Reading people had become a part of him just as breathing. Since the beginning he couldn't quite place her. Something about her bothers him and he can't quite put his finger on it.

Abby shouldn't be bothering him but she does and he doesn't like it. Why did he offer to take her home? Why didn't he listen to her and drop her off at the bus stop? His conscience is telling him that his inquisitiveness has got the better of him yet he wants to know more about her. He got his wish and did find out more about her, but what he found out should have frightened him away because of the things he has heard about the area in which she lives. The women there earn their money in a very different manor, which he does not agree with.

A devil's thought appears in his mind, maybe she's one of them. He must admit she is a very beautiful woman with a sexy body and why wouldn't she use it to her advantage. He glances over at her, but she looks so innocent and young, then again looks can be deceiving. Maybe I should give her the benefit of the doubt.

On a wall in front of them appears the name Hantom park, it is Abby's apartment block. The block of flats is much neglected and Cal stops the car with the engine running. He looks at the block of flats and can't help but notice how worn down it is.

Abby's good manners stop her from getting out of the car. She opens the door, looks him straight in the eye and with frost in her eyes she thanks him. She struggles along on her one leg and looks for her keys in her bag. Abby opens her front door and hears the car pull out and drive away. She closes the door behind her. She moves toward the kitchen and scratches in the freezer for a bag of ice. She switches on the kettle, then takes the ice and sits down on the couch.

She pulls the coffee table towards her and rests her foot on it. Her foot is throbbing but she tries not to think about it. She looks around her and everything catches her eye. Even thou the apartment is small and simple, it is always neat and tidy. Jimmy knows to put his toys away once he has finished playing with them. In the lounge are two couches with green throws. Yellow and orange pillows create a feeling of warmth. The walls are painted white, a big clock as well as a few portraits parading on the walls. The sliding door that leads to the back yard is covered with yellow curtains. The kitchen is small and allows room for only a stove, fridge, sink, a row of shelves and a small counter for work space. Against the wall opposite the kitchen are two doors. The first door leads to the bathroom, with only a basin, toilet and bath. The second door leads to a bedroom that was first hers but she now shares it with Jimmy.

The kettle boils and Abby gets up to make her tea. She takes out some pain relievers from the medicine cabinet. She takes her tea and pain relievers to go and sit on the couch. She takes the pain relievers and finishes her tea. She lies back and closes her eyes.

A while later she opens her eyes and gasps at the time. She has been sleeping for almost two hours. The apartment is quite and empty. Then she realises she still needs to fetch Jimmy from Aunt Ella next door. Abby gets up and move easier because most of the pain is gone now.

The front door bell rings and Aunt Ella gets up to answer it. She opens the door and greets Abby with a smile: "Afternoon dear, come in. Take a seat, Jimmy is still sleeping in my bed. I'll make some tea. Abby frowns and asks:" Sleep, this time of the day?"

"He's only been sleeping for about a half an hour, he told me that he is tired and because you mentioned earlier that he had a bad night's sleep, I took him to my room and let him sleep."

"Yes it's true he did not sleep well last night. I had a look at his medical card and noticed that he has an appointment tomorrow. The doctor should be able to tell me when they can remove Jimmy's tonsils."

"The sooner the better."

Abby enters the apartment and Aunt Ella realises that she is limping.

"What happened to your foot, dear?"

Abby takes a seat at the wooden table and pulls a sour face as she talks: "Aunt Ella you won't believe what I went through this morning."

"Let me switch on the kettle, and then you can tell me all about it."

With a cup of warm tea Abby tells Aunt Ella about everything that happened this morning. Aunt Ella sits and listens attentively but tries to keep a straight face about the spider. She can see that Abby is still upset about it. "Did you get the job?"

"The interview was never completed so, I doubt it."

"Abby my dear just keep the faith, at least you still have the job at the restaurant." Abby puts a good face on and says: "That's true although I really needed that job." Aunt Ella changes the subject: "How's the foot feeling."

"I've taken a pain reliever, still struggling to put my weight on it but I'm sure it will be fine by tomorrow."

"Dear, if it's not fine by tomorrow, I'll take Jimmy to the doctor." Abby shakes her head profoundly and says: "No Aunt Ella, I can't expect you to do that you are already doing so much for us. During the day you look after Jimmy and stand in for me when I go to interviews, thank you for offering but I can't abuse your kind heartedness."

"Abby my dear, I love both and Jimmy very much as if you were my own, don't ever think that you are misusing my kindness. I know you worried about my health, but I would never have offered if I wasn't feeling up to it." Abby is still not convinced but what is she to do she may have to accept Aunt Ella's offer if her foot is not doing better tomorrow.

She takes her last sip, stands up, walks around the table and gives Aunt Ella a big hug: "Thank you for all of your help, what would I do without you?"

Cal tosses and turns in his bed struggling to fall asleep. He walks to the kitchen to get a glass of water. With one gulp he finishes the glass of water and pours another. He takes the glass and walks to the lounge of his penthouse. Looking out the window at the stars in the night sky. Normally he would enjoy looking at the stars but not tonight . . . . As a child he was fascinated by the moon and the stars.

He always imagined that if he reaches out far enough he would be able to touch it. The moon and the stars always reminded him a powerful force. No matter who or where you are you would always have to look up to them. He promised himself that one day he would also have that kind of power. Everybody would look up to and admire him for what he has accomplished in life.

He took an oath that he would never be like his father. After his father wasted all of his inheritance on women and booze, he walked out on them, never to return. They lead a dog's life after his father's betrayal.

His mother had to look for work to keep support herself and eleven year old son. She got a job as a receptionist with an Engineering firm. She was a beautiful woman and used it to her advantage to get what she wanted. Not long after about a month or so, she married a director of the firm. Tough Elizabeth was extremely happy about her good fortune. Marring the millionaire Ray Conner who was a good husband but never in any way father figure for Cal. When the time came for Cal to go to high school Ray convinced Elizabeth that it was in Cal's best interest to be sent to boarding school.

She didn't think twice about sending him, but Cal wasn't interested in going. Elizabeth shouted at her son that she would do anything to keep Ray happy so if that meant he must go to boarding school then so be it. The day that Elizabeth dropped Cal off at the boarding school was the last time her ever saw his mother. His roommate Mark Bailey was and still is his best friend. It's with him that Cal went home every weekend and it was his parents that encouraged Cal to study further after graduation.

Cal turns away from the window and takes a seat on the sofa. He can't stop thinking about the women he met this morning. He can still feel her in his arms and taste her soft lips. He feels his body reacting towards the thought of her and quarrels with himself: "Come on Cal get a hold of yourself! It's a bad woman with bad habits. You can't let her get the better of you." Exhausted he leans back and closes his eyes, he sees a vision of her and it's not a pleasant one. She stands on the centre of the stage, in front of a pole, wearing a black lace bra and panty barely covering it all. The stage is surrounded by a group of men with dirty thoughts, each of them waiting their turn to have their way with her. She looks down at them, not with a smile but with devastation written all over her face. He shakes his head vigorously, trying to get rid of these thoughts, but her devastated face is imprinted in his mind. It's as if she is begging him to help her escape from these hungry wolves.

The feeling to protect her won't subside. While pacing he is trying to convince himself: "Are you crazy Cal. She will only cause trouble. Not physically but emotionally. This is not the type of person you should get involved with yet alone bring her into the company." Suddenly he comes to a Holt and realises that he never completed the interview. His conscious tells him you think of yourself as a righteous man, therefore everybody deserves a fair chance. You should not let your personal feelings get in the way of a business decision. Cal then decides he will in fact give her the benefit of the doubt. It's the only way he will be able to determine whether he was right or wrong. He will personally inform her that her application has been successful.

As soon as he find evidence that proves he was right about her he will ask her to leave. After all he is a lawyer and when he draws up the employment contract he will make sure that she is of no obligation towards the company. Satisfied with his decision he returns to his bed.

Chapter 4

Friday morning Abby wakes up to the sound of the alarm. She attempts to get up. As she steps on her foot the pain shoots up in her leg and she falls back onto the bed again. On the other side if the room is Jimmy's bed he is still sleeping soundly.

Abby carefully get up again struggles over to Jimmy's bed. She looks down at the sleeping boy and strokes his check lightly with the back of her hand. He seems to have a bit of a temperature so she bends over using her lips to determine if he has a fever or not. She whispers to him: "We are going to the doctor shortly and he will give us medicine to take away all your aches and pains. It's almost as if Jimmy hears Abby talking to him. He lifts his head pecking through the cracks of his eyelids. "Good morning my Sweetheart. Did you sleep well?" Jimmy's eyes are wide open and he stretches. "Is it mornin awready mus I get up?"

Abby gets up carefully and smiles at him. "Yes sweetheart its morning and you must get up now. Aunt Ella will be here shortly and you need to eat porridge before you go to the doctor." Jimmy is sitting up straight in his bed and with question in his eyes: "Were we went the other day?" Abby laughs and scruffs her fingers through his hair: "Yes were we where the other day. He is going to see why you are getting so sick why the medicine is not working." Jimmy is not making any attempts to get up his thoughts are with the medicine and the doctor that Abby spoke about. Abby looks at Jimmy and notices that he is a bit unsure of what's happening.

"You're not scared of a doctor are you?" So many questions are running through his mind. Since the last time he was at the doctor, he's been thinking a lot about his mother. Jimmy jumps out of bed and is very excited when he starts talking: "I know bout docors and mootie and I'm not scawed. Mommy always gives me mootie when I cough. She says it will make me feel bette. Is mommy awso a docor?" Jimmy is out of breath. Shocked Abby stands and looks at Jimmy. It's the first time since Jimmy arrived that he has spoken about his mother.

Without answering him she turns and walks towards the kitchen. Memories of Cathy start filling her mind. She remembers how they used to play, despite the fact that they were so different they were still very close. She pushes her hands against her head as if she was trying to push the memories out of her mind. The she hears Jimmy ask again: "Was mommy a docor?" Abby ignores the question completely and says: "Go sit at the table and eat your porridge." Jimmy wants to say something again but rather does what Abby told him to. Jimmy thinks to himself, Latew I will go to Aunt Ella and ask her. She will tell me evewythin I want to know.

Eight thirty Jimmy is dressed. He and Abby are waiting in the lounge for Aunt Ella to arrive. There is a knock on the door and Jimmy jumps up to open it. Abby taught him to always ask before he opens the door and so he does: "Who is theer?" Aunt Ella answers that it's her and Jimmy opens the door. She smiles widely at him and he hugs her tightly.

"Morning my dear, did you sleep well?" He nods his head and she glances over at Abby: "Morning my dear, Abby, how's the foot feeling?"

"Morning Aunt Ella, it's still very sore. I can't even step on it" Aunt Ella takes a seat on the couch across from Abby. Jimmy closes the door and takes a seat next to Aunt Ella. Aunt Ella looks worried and says to Abby: "You will also have to go to the doctor if your foot doesn't get better soon."

"I'm sure I'll be okay, just give it another day or two. I won't be able to go in to work today but I'll just let them know, I'm sure they will be fine with it." Again there is a knock on the door, Jimmy jumps up and wants to answer but Abby stops him. She frowns wondering who it could be, Aunt Ella noticed it. "Are you expecting someone?"

"No, not at all."

Aunt Ella gets up to see who it is. Standing at the door she asks who it is. A bubbly voice answers: "It's me Sally may I come in?" Aunt Ella opens the door. With a wide smile on her red painted lips, Sally greets her: "Hi Aunt Ella, It's lovely to see you again!"

Sally is a blonde haired woman, well groomed and very wealthy. She and Abby have been friends since Abby started working at the restaurant. Sally work for her father and his business is in the building next to the restaurant. Sally comes in every afternoon to buy lunch, that's how they met and soon after became friends.

Aunt Ella once said to Jimmy that Sally is as mad as a hatter. Jimmy didn't understand what she meant by it, but the word Hatter stuck with him. Ever since that day he calls Sally Aunt Hatty. It doesn't seem to bother Sally. Jimmy and Sally have a very good relationship.

"Is Abby's in?"

Abby is surprised to see her best friend: "Hi Sally. What are you doing here? I thought you said you have to go to Cape Town for a course?"

"The course has been postponed until next month." Sally walks past the old lady, straight to Jimmy. She grabs him, picks him up and gives him a big kiss on his cheek. From experience Jimmy knows there is a big red lipstick mark on his cheek and while he tries to wipe it off he pulls his face. "Aunt Hatty don't kiss me wiff your wred mouf." Sally looks like she is very hurt by what he has just said, puts her hand on her heart and lets out a big groan. She cuddles up next to Abby on the couch, still focusing on Jimmy. "Where are you going that you're all dressed up, Cheeky Chop?"

"I'm goin to the docor cause I am sick."

"The doctor is going to give you an injection."

"Nooooo, he's gonna gime mootie."

"Injections are mootie. He just uses a long thick needle to get it in your system."

Abby gives Sally a fat smack on her thigh. "Ouch, what was that for?"

"Don't make him scared of the doctor, Sally!"

Sally can't let an opportunity pass by when it comes to teasing Jimmy. Even so Abby, Sally and Jimmy have a special bond.

Sally looks at her friend and notices that she is still in her pyjamas. "Why aren't you dressed yet? Aren't you going with him to the doctor?"

"No Aunt Ella is going to take him, I sprained my foot yesterday and I can't step on it."

"What happened?" Sally looks concerned.

"Oh, it's a long story."

"I'll make tea and you can tell me all about it." Abby knows that if Sally wants to know something she keeps on and on until she has the answer. So she would have to tell her eventually. While Sally goes to the kitchen, Aunt Ella gets up as says to Jimmy: "Come, Come Jimmy we have quite a way to walk." Sally turns throws her hands in the air and looks disgusted: "Walk did hear correctly, Walk to the doctor?" Sally looks at Abby with accusation in her eyes. Abby wanted to explain but

Sally doesn't want to give her a chance: "Shame on you Abs! How can you let Aunt Ella walk so far?" Aunt Ella jumps in while pointing towards Abby's foot: "I offered to take Jimmy to the doctor. If Abby had to do it they would probably have taken the whole day."

"She could have asked me, I would have done it with pleasure." She turns to Abby and asks: "Is my car not good enough for you?" Abby rolls her eyes: "Oh come on Sally, do you have to be so mellowing dramatic, I didn't ask you because you were supposed to be in Cape Town for a course. Was I supposed to smell it was postponed?" Sally being just as sarcastic replies: "Abby, sarcasm is the lowest form of wit, I'm hear know so I can take him. What time is the appointment?"

"Nine thirty."

Sally looks at the clock on the wall: "We will need to get a move on Jimmy, the traffic this time of the morning is terrible." Jimmy doesn't understand what Sally is referring to when she talks about traffic but gets up and puts the jacket on that Abby handed to him.

Suddenly a thought comes to Aunt Ella's mind: "Abby why don't you accompany them, maybe the doctor can squeeze you in. Your foot is really swollen it wouldn't hurt just to ask." Everyone is staring at Abby's swollen foot and Sally pipes up: "Yes, I think Aunt Ella is right. Abby you have 15 minute to get done." Abby looks at Sally: "I don't even have an appointment, who says he will be able to squeeze me in." Abby says this not because of the appointment but actually because she doesn't have enough money to pay for the appointment and is too proud to admit it to anyone of the two women and she knows if she does they would offer to help and she doesn't want to have to owe anybody anything.

Sally replies: "Abby don't worry about the appointment, you go and get done Jimmy and I will be waiting outside in the car. She takes Jimmy's hand and off they go to the car.

Chapter 5

Cal knocks on Abby's front door but nobody answers. He knocks again just harder and still nobody answers. He wonders where she could be. Aunt Ella hears the banging and walks towards her front door to see what all the fuss is about. She opens the door and looks straight into broad shoulders. I wonder who this could be, Abby doesn't have male friends: "Excuse me Sir, can I help you? Cal turn and sees and elderly lady standing in from of him: "I'm looking for Ms Spence, do you perhaps know where I can find her?"

"She not in at the moment, she's gone to the doctor."

"I see, do you know when she will return?"

"She shouldn't be long." Aunt Ella hesitates: "If you would like, I can give her a message."

"No thank you, I'll try again later."

Cal greets her and walks to his car. Aunt Ella looks at the man as he drives away and thinks out loud. "Who is this good looking man that is look for Abby?"

Abby and Jimmy walk into the doctor's rooms. The doctor notices them and gets up from behind his desk. He walks towards them, with his hand extended gives her friendly greeting. He sees Abby is limping and asks: "Why are you limping?"

"I fell over my own feet, doctor."

The doctor bends down and lifts the leg of her trousers up. He looks at her injury:" As soon as I'm done with Mr Jay, I'll have a proper look. It doesn't look to serious though."

"Thank you Doctor."

The doctor rises to his feet and pat's Jimmy on the head while saying: "Good Morning Mr Jay, and how are you this morning?" Jimmy looks up at him and smiles: "Not so good docor, I not feelin well."

"Jump on the bed so long Mr J; I'll be with you in a second."

Jimmy jumps on the bed and sits quietly waiting for the doctor. Child like eyes looks around the room absorbing as much as possible. Abby stands next to Jimmy and takes his hand in hers. Jimmy pulls his hand away. "You don't have to hold my hand, I'm not scawed." Abby and the doctor laugh at how brave Jimmy is being.

The doctor stand in front of Jimmy: "Right Mr Jay let's see, open your mouth as wide as possible." Jimmy does what the doctor asks. While the doctor is busy with his examination Abby takes a seat on one of the chairs next to the bed. She is worried about her finances and how much the next round of medication is going to cost her. Since Jimmy became sick she had to cut back on a lot of things. She has to think twice before she can spend a cent. She doesn't even have a cent to by Jimmy a sweet.

She really needed to get that job yesterday so that she could make ends meet. She would have worked there during the day and then have more time with Jimmy in the evenings and over weekends. The doctors words bring her back to the now. "There we go Mr Jay we are all done." Jimmy gets off the bed and stands next to Abby. The doctor walks to his desk and opens his draw, he takes out a lollipop and hands it too Jimmy." This is for you for being such a good patient." Jimmy is so impressed with this big lollipop, he rips the paper off and shoves it in his mouth. Abby taps him on his shoulder. "What do you say?"

"Thank you, Doctor."

"The pleasure is mine, I hope you enjoy it."

Jimmy disappears into the passage and walks towards Aunt Hatty. Sally sees him and tells him to come and sit next to her. "Where is Abb's?"

"She's still in the doctor's room." He points to the door. Sally points to the lollipop and asks: "And this where did you get that?"

"The docor gave it to me."

"Give me a bite." Sally leans to take the lollipop from his hand.

"Noooooo!!! Leave my lolli, the docor gave it to me it's mine."

Sally pulls a face and he laughs.

The doctor looks Abby in the eyes. "Ms I see on the previous report that he had tonsillitis but the tonsils look perfectly fine to me. Although the throat is red and the lymphatic nodes in the lower jaw are swollen, it points to a throat infection. Does he complain of a sore throat?"

"No doctor." The doctor takes a prescription pad out of his draw and starts writing. When he completed his prescription he explained to Abby what he wrote. "I have prescribed an antibiotic it is a 10 day course and must be completed. The description on the bottle explains the dosage. Come back in ten days time."

"Thank you doctor, I will do so."

"It my pleasure Ms, let's take a look at that foot." The doctor shows her to the bed and she gets on. He rolls up the leg of her trousers and examines the sore foot. He pushes on a few spots and he shakes his head. "As I said earlier the injury is not that serious you have just sprained your ankle. I am going to put an ointment on it and cover it up with a bandage.

Doctor Grey, walks towards the medical cabinet and opens it, he takes out the ointment and bandage and closes the cupboards, with the two items in hand her walks back to Abby. He puts it on the table next to the bed.

He lifts her foot and rubs in the ointment then he carefully covers the foot with a bandage.

When he was finished he looks at her and says: "As soon as the swelling has gone down and you feel that you can walk on it again you can remove the bandage."

"Thanks for your trouble, Doctor."

"It's no trouble, it's a great pleasure."

Abby gets off the bed and thanks the doctor again while walking towards the door. She opens the door tilts her head and greets him. "Good bye doctor."

"Good bye don't forget to make an appointment with the receptionist. I want to see him in 10 days time."

Aunt Ella must have heard the car stop. As they got out of the car Aunt Ella was already standing at the front door. She sees the bandage on Abby's foot and is happy the doctor could squeeze her in. They walk towards Aunt Ella, and Jimmy speaks first:" Hello Aunt Ella, look at my big lolli."

"Shoe, but that's a big lollipop Jimmy, were did you get that?"

"At the docor he says I was wery good and I wasn't even scawed."

Aunt Ella walks towards Jimmy and holds him tightly while she says:" I am glad to hear that you were such a brave boy." She invited all three of them to come in for some coffee.

Jimmy and Sally walk through the sliding door leading to the back garden. He shows Sally were Aunt Ella planted the bulbs and were he took out the weeds.

Aunt Ella puts the kettle on and sits next to Abby on one of the comfortable chairs. "What did the doctor say dear? When are they going to remove his tonsils?"

"The tonsils are not going to be removed, according to the doctor it was never tonsillitis it was a throat infection." Aunt Ella frowns and asks: "How is that possible, dear?" Abby sighs and tells Aunt Ella everything that the doctor said. Aunt Ella shrugs her shoulders and says:" Well we can only hope that the medication works and he gets better soon. The poor child is suffering with all these sicknesses that don't seem to want to get better.

Abby remember her foot and lifts it for Aunt Ella to see the bandage. "The doctor was so kind he had a look at my foot as well. He applied an ointment and covered it with a bandage. He says as soon as can step on it, I can take off the bandage."

"I noticed when you got out of the car, I am glad he sorted it out for you." Aunt Ella looks at Abby and smiles. She remembers the man that was there earlier and mentions it to Wilma. As Aunt Ella expected, Abby was very surprised to hear about the mysterious visitor. "Did they not leave a name or mention why they were here or what they wanted?"

"I asked but he said he will come back later."

Cal's face appears in the back of her mind and she feels butterflies in her stomach. She immediately erases the idea that it could be him out of her mind. It couldn't have been him, what would he be doing here?" A feeling of disappointment flows through her and she can't understand why. Aunt Ella puts Abby's cup of coffee down on a small side table next to her. "Thank you Aunt Ella."

Aunt Ella stands at the sliding door and calls Sally and Jimmy to come get there juice and coffee. Sally and Jimmy came inside to get the drinks that Aunt Ella poured them. Sally takes a seat on the couch and pulls Jimmy on her lap. "Come sit here with me. I want to ask you something."

"What do you want to ask me Aunt Hatty?" Sally looks very deep in thought. "Do you know what special day is around the corner?" Jimmy doesn't have a clue what she is talking about. "I donno."

"What do you mean you don't know . . . . ? It's almost Christmas." Jimmy's eyes and sparkling with joy as her says: "Christmas."

"What would you like for Christmas, cheeky chop?"

"You can't awsk me, I may not say, otherwise fader Christmas won't give it to me. Littwl chirdren must wite a lettew and send it to him only he may know what I want."

"Father Christmas asked me to ask you what you want for Christmas. He can't get to all the children there are to many. That is why he gets some people to help him." Sally is very impressed with the quick answer she came up with. Jimmy on the other hand wasn't quite sure if he should trust her. He asks: "Are you one of Santa's helpers?"

"A what?"

"No you'we not cause you don't even know what it is."

Abby and Aunt Ella sit and watch the two of them. They wonder how Abby is going to talk her way out of this one. She surprises them again with her answer: "Man, I know what Santa's helpers are, I just couldn't hear what you said, and you must learn to open your mouth." Jimmy looks at her and asks again: "What is Santa's Helper?"

"Santa's Helpers are elves that help Santa make toys for all the children around the world." Jimmy absorbs everything that Sally is telling him, confused he asks: "No!"

"What, why are you saying No?"

"Cause you awe not small, you are big and all Santa's helpers awe small!"

Aunt Ella and Abby are enjoying how Jimmy is taking a stand for what he believes in. Sally looks a bit hurt. She looks at him with amusement and says: "You can't write so how is Father Christmas going to know what you want for Christmas?"

"I awe gonna dwaw a pictuwe, fathew Christmas is vewy clewer he knows what children want."

Sally wanted to say something, but decided to keep quite when she saw the scorn in Aunt Ella and Abby's eyes.

Abby sees Sally wants to say something and says: "No way Sally, you'll have to give up, he saw right through you."

Sally pulls a face and laughs.

"Ok then, you'll have to draw your picture soon, there are a lot of children and there is very little time left for Santa to go through it all.

Chapter 6

Abby bends over Jimmy to give him a good night kiss. Strangely enough she has had no problems getting him into bed the last few days. Lately he tells her that he is tired or he falls asleep on the couch and then she takes him to his bed. Abby sits on the edge of the bed.

She is looking at him and thinking to herself, shame it's probably the medicine that is making him so tired or maybe it's because he doesn't sleep well at night. She is just happy that the doctor has pin pointed the infection and the medication he has prescribed works.

She feels very sorry for Jimmy because he doesn't really understand why he has to stay with her. Abby knows it's her fault that he doesn't understand. She should have told him about the accident but how can she? He can barely talk never mind understand.

The day that she needed to go and identify the bodies, she flat out refused. She still cannot accept their death. She also didn't go to the funeral because that would mean that she would have to acknowledge that they had passed. Sometimes she finds herself waiting for their arrival and the tears run down her face.

She almost has to put her fist to stop from sobbing. Abby stands up and walks to the bathroom to wash her face. She then goes to the lounge and sits on the couch. Abby had barely sat down when she hears a knock on the door. She looks at the clock on the wall, it's not eight o' clock yet so it could be Aunt Ella. She opens the door and her heart skips a beet or two she expected the devil before she would expect him. Abby almost chocked on her words: "You, what would you be doing here at this time of the evening?" Cal didn't expect her to be overwhelmed with joy; neither did he expect her to be so antagonistic. "Good evening Ms Spence, I was here earlier today but your neighbour advised me that you had gone to the doctor, I decided to come back a bit later." Abby sounds very cynical: "Very much later, I would say. What can I do for you Mr Blake?"

Cal isn't bothered by her cynical and antagonistic attitude. He walks straight past her into the apartment. Abby wants to go into a fit of rage by the way he arrogantly imposes on her privacy.

The only way that she can get him out is by using force or shouting at him. She can't use force on him as she is not a violent person. She can't yell at him because Jimmy will wake up. She has no other choice but to listen to what he has to say if she doesn't like what she hears then she will show him the door.

Cal made himself at home on one of the couches and waited patiently for her to join him. He looks at the room and notices that it is very neat and tidy, to his surprise he actually like the colours that she has used and feels quite at home. The apartment is not what he had imagined but then again what did he imagine.

He expected something else and was very surprised to find that he was wrong about her. Okay he advises himself, it's not to say that because her apartment gets my approval, that her lifestyle and profession will get my approval as well. Before Abby takes a seat she closes the bedroom door. Cal notices it and he gets a feeling that she knows what she is doing. "Don't worry Ms Spence; I'm not interested in snooping around in your bedroom, if that's why you're closing your door."

Abby glares at him. "For your information I'm not closing my door because I think you're going to snoop around, I'm closing it because there is someone sleeping in the bedroom who I don't wish to wake up." Cal can't help himself and asks: "Is it a special person?" What has it got to do with him who is in the room and who does he think is in the room, Abby thinks to herself. My personal life has got nothing to do with him. She decides to say it: "I can't see what it's got to do with you but yes it is someone special, very special."

She knows that he might be making his own assumption, but she doesn't care if that's what he wants to do then let him. She didn't lie; Jimmy is sleeping in his room and is very special to her. Of course he is special to her he is all that she has left. No, Abby No, your family is still alive they are on their way, you must have faith it's the only thing that has kept you going for the past six months.

She thinks to herself. Abby pushes the thoughts aside and takes a seat on the couch opposite Cal. Cal sees her foot bandaged up and asks: "How's the foot?"

Abby looks at him and says: "It still pains when I step on it, but I'll live." There is a silence in the room making Abby feel uncomfortable. The electricity between the two in the room is powerful. Abby's feels butterflies in her stomach while looking at his lips and she thinks about the kiss they shared yesterday. She has no resistance when it comes to Cal. He looks at her and the silence is causing tension between them.

Abby realises that he has not yet mentioned the reason for his visit. She takes a deep breath and asks: "I'm sure you are not here to discuss my personal life or my health, so why are you really here? Mr Blake." Cal looks at her with amusement in his eyes: "Don't you offer your guest something to drink?" Abby goes to the kitchen, she puts on the kettle and gets the cups ready.

Cal's thoughts wonder back to the special person that Abby had mentioned. Although he was the one that kissed her, he is almost certain that she kissed him back. However he can't understand why she kissed him back. He thinks about the kiss again and he is certain that she surrendered herself to the kiss.

But the thought of the special person won't leave his mind because it means that she was unfaithful to that person. For some reason he can't stop thinking about the person in the room. It can't be her husband because there is no sign of a ring or even a tan line that would indicate there was a ring. It has to be a boyfriend, but why would he be sleeping so early?

He looks at his wrist watch and sees that it's just after eight. He's probably an angry drunk, that's why she doesn't want to wake him. Cal sees a vision of the drunken hitting Abby and a sudden rage comes upon him. The feeling to protect her has changed into an impulse that he doesn't understand and has never felt before. He tries very hard to give the feeling a name but the only name he could come up with is jealousy, He was jealous of Abby's boyfriend. Jealous, he asks himself, how can you be jealous of a man you have never seen before?

A voice in his head corrects him. He is not jealous of the man himself he is jealous of the thought of another man. He tries to smother the voice in his head and convince himself that he doesn't want her and he isn't jealous. You liar, you have desired her since the day she walked into your office. "No"

"Excuse me?"

Cal realises that he must have spoken out loud and he waves off. "It's nothing, really." Abby looks at Cal and frowns. She wonders, what is the matter with him? Why is he talking to himself?

She puts the cups, sugar and milk in a tray, she wants to pick it up but he takes it out of her hands and places it on the coffee table. When walking past her he brushes up against her. It makes her week in the knees. Her legs feel like jelly her quickly takes a seat on the couch. Cal picks up a cup and without looking at her asks her how many sugars and if she takes milk in her coffee.

He hands her the coffee, takes his cup and sits down on the couch. He sips on his coffee and looks her straight in the eye as he says: "We need to talk about what happened yesterday." Abby looks at him and just the mention of what happened makes her blush and Cal notices it. How can he tell her it was a mistake, if he wants it to happen again? She looks charming with her black curls hanging wildly on her shoulders.

He feels hypnotised by her big green eyes staring at him. His mouth dries up just looking at her blush. She takes his breath away. He opens his mouth to say something but closes it again without saying a word. He sees she looks over at the closed bedroom door and it spoils the passion right there.

He clears his throat before he starts talking. "Ms Spence, I realised that the interview didn't go as smoothly as we would have liked, but I do believe that everyone deserves a fair chance, we also contacted the restaurant and they said it would be a loss to the company if we didn't hire you." He keeps quite and takes a sip of his coffee.

Abby pinches herself to make sure that she is awake. He follows with:" I decided to inform you personally that we don't want to have the loss in not hiring you. Abby almost messes the coffee all over her in shock.

She looks at him surprisingly. "Are you . . . saying . . . that I . . . got the . . . . job?" Cal could not get over the look of surprise on her face. In a strange way it gives him pleasure to see her absolutely dumbfounded. He gets the feeling that she hasn't had much good news lately. "Yes Ms Spence, you have got the job."

Abby still can't believe what she has just heard. It's such a relief that she feels like bursting into tears. She blinks her eyes and the tears disappear. He will never know about the weight he lifted off her shoulders tonight but she will always be grateful to him. Abby swallows and says: "Thank you very much. When would you like me too start?"

"As soon as you foot has healed you can come into the office."

"It should be fine by Monday. The doctor said as soon as I can step on my foot I can take off the bandage. It normally takes about 2 or 3 days."

"Let's make it Tuesday, and then your foot has enough time to heal properly."

Cal finishes his coffee and takes the empty cups along with the coffee tray to the kitchen. Abby gets up and looks at Cal, He is standing with his back towards her. Cal turns to greet her but he feels like words have failed him when he sees the way she is looking at him.

Their eyes meet, in less than moments he finds himself standing in front of her. He takes her into his arms and then he kisses her. The first kiss was passionate and it felt like she was flying, this kiss was hard and aggressive her lips feel sore. After a while the aggression subsides and turns into hunger.

She feels the lust he is kissing her with and it is very overwhelming. She puts her arms around his neck and kisses him with the same lustfulness he has shown. Abby's not sure how long it lasted and the next moment her pushes her away like she has a deadly disease, losing her balance she falls back onto the coach and he disappears into the black night.

She is so disorientated that she doesn't realise what just happened. She gets up in daze and closes the front door. Later that night lying in her bed she tries to figure out what went wrong.

First he was kissing her like she is the only women alive and the next he is pushing her away as if he has made the biggest mistake of his life. Abby is so confused, not only with the kiss but with the feelings it woke up inside of her. All these feelings are strange to her and she is searching for the right word to call it. While busy thinking, she hears Jimmy calling her. "Abby, my neck is sowe."

She turns on the lamp. She gets up and sits on next to Jimmy on his bed. Once again she rubs her lips on his forehead to check his temperature. He seems to be very warm. She goes to the kitchen and gets the thermometer. "Abby!"

"I'm coming Jimmy, I'm trying to find the thermometer."

He calls again, but this time he is anxious: "Abby."

"I'm coming. Damn were did I put that thermometer, Oh here it is. Thank goodness."

With the thermometer in her hand she walks as quickly as possible to the room. "Sorry I took so long but . . . ." She stops dead in her tracks and with a shocked look on her face, she looks at the boy lying in the bed. "Jimmy!" She rushes over to him. "What hap . . . . ? Why is your nose bleeding? Did you scratch in it?" With tears running down his face he answers: "No I didn't it just stawted bleedin." Abby sighs. "Its ok sweetheart, I'll be right back, I'm just going to fetch some tissues to wipe your nose." In less than no time she returns with the tissues in her hand. She takes her place next to him on the bed, helps him to sit up straight and says: "Jimmy, I'm going to need you to lean forward while I pinch your nose closed. I need you to breathe through your mouth, are you okay with that?" Jimmy nods his head and Abby pinches his nose closed. While she is holding it she questions why his nose started bleeding. After a while she slowly lets go of the nose and luckily the bleeding has stopped. She holds him closer and says: "its ok my sweetheart it's only a bit of blood let's put on a new pair of pyjama's these ones have blood on them."

"Can I sleep wif you in your bed?"

"Of course you can, once we have taken off those bloody pyjamas."

He lifts his arms up above his head so that she can take off the top and his pants follow. With a smile she says: "Why don't you get into bed while I soak these cloths."

Jimmy gets into Abby's bed. Abby goes to the bathroom and fills the basin with water. She puts the clothes in the basin along with some washing powder. "It can soak like this till the morning." She puts off the light and goes back to the bedroom. Abby sees Jimmy fast asleep in bed and she gets in next to him. She turns off the light and gives him a goodnight kiss.

Chapter 7

It's Saturday morning and Abby struggles to get out of bed. Her foot is not paining as much anymore but she is very tired. She thinks about what happened through the night and remembers the pyjamas are still lying in the basin. She will have to wash it and hang it outside. Abby looks over at Jimmy who is fast asleep, she carefully gets out of bed trying not to wake him.

She tip toes to the bathroom and washes the clothes. She then goes outside to hang them up. Just before she could enter the apartment again she hears someone call her name. "Morning Abby, dear." Abby turns to find Aunt Ella working in her garden. "Oh Morning Aunt Ella." She waves at her. Aunt Ella walks towards the fence separating the two apartments.

She notices the clothes that Abby hung up and asks: "Did our angel have a little mishap last night?" Abby sighs "If you can call a bleeding nose a mishap, then yes he had one."

"Come again, whose nose bled?"

"Jimmy's." She then tells Aunt Ella all about what happened.

"Shame poor child is he still sleeping?"

"Yes Aunt Ella, I'll leave him to let him sleep. I can't understand how it happened that his nose started bleeding. I asked him if he may have scratched in his nose or bumped it, but he says he didn't."

"That's very strange; maybe he bumped it while he was sleeping without realising it. It won't necessarily start bleeding immediately." Abby doesn't look very convinced but she will have to be satisfied with that explanation. "Maybe your right, these things happen."

"Well Abby dear, why don't you turn on the kettle while I wash my hands and I'll come over for some tea?"

"I'll do so." Abby disappears into her apartment.

She goes to the kitchen and turns on the kettle. She opens then front door and goes back to the kitchen waiting for the kettle to boil.

Aunt Ella arrives just in time for the tea. "Are we going to have the tea outside in the garden Aunt Ella?"

"Yes why not, it's such a lovely morning."

Abby places the two cups with sugar and milk on the tray. Aunt Ella picks up the tray and says: "While I take the tea outside. I suggest you close the front door and don't forget to lock it, these days you can't leave it open, any Tom, Dick and Harry could walk in and who knows what they might do to you."

With a smile on Abby's face she walks towards the door closes it and locks it. She then accompanies Aunt Ella outside in the garden. She takes the tea Aunt Ella poured for her and asks: "Why are you so concerned about locking the front door?" Aunt Ella takes a sip of her tea and answers: "My mother always said better safe than sorry." Abby has no idea where this is leading to and asks: "Aunt Ella, Where is all of this coming from?"

"Haven't you heard about what happened to old lady Fisher?"

"No, did something happen to her?"

"Yes, it was terrible. Everybody always warned her about leaving the front door wide open but she didn't listen. The other day she was in her kitchen baking some cookies. When she looked up there were two strange men standing in the middle of her lounge. You must remember she is in her late ninety's and not always all there, if you know what I mean. Do you know what she did, she offered them something to eat and drink." Abby being very attentive asks: "Really?"

"Yes and it just shows you how conceited thieves of today are. They first enjoy their tea party and afterwards they strap her to a chair and then they cleaned out the place." Abby, fascinated by the story asks: "And then?"

"What do you mean by and?"

"Well, did they catch the thieves and what happened to the stuff they stole? Did she get anything back?"

"Never will she never see those things again."

"How did she get loose from the chair?"

"Old John from next door, His grandchildren went over to her to get something sweet, that's when they found her tied up to the chair. Instead of untying her or asking for help from one of the other residents, they ran all the way to John's work, to tell him he must come and help."

"Isn't John's work down town? Why run all the way down there?"

"No, Abby, I won't be able to answer you, you never know what is going through their little minds."

Abby can't stop herself from laughing: "I can't believe that happened. It sounds so impractical, during the day there is so much movement in that area" Aunt Ella replies: "If it can happen their then it can happen here to, so just in case keep your doors locked at all times."

"Thank you for the warning, but I don't think I have anything they would want to steel. I can offer them coffee or tea but that's about it."

Aunt Ella is upset and says: "Abby stop it, it's not something to joke about." Aunt Ella changes the subject: "How is your foot this morning?"

"Much better Thank you for asking. I can almost put my weight on it, I'm sure I'll be able to stand on it tomorrow."

"Don't be over keen, give the foot time to heal completely."

A moment of silence follows while they drink there tea. Abby remembers the visitor she had last night. Abby so excited she could jump out her seat says to her: "Aunt Ella, you will never guess what happened to me last night." Aunt Ella was so startled by Abby's outburst she spilt the last bit of tea in her cup out on the table.

"Abby, look what you have done, you gave me such a fright I spilt my tea all over the table. With remorse Abby says to Aunt Ella: "I'm so sorry, I didn't mean to startle you. Let me fetch a cloth to clean up this mess." Off she goes to the kitchen. Abby comes back with the cloth, wipes the table, rings out the cloth and hangs it up on the washing line. "I'm really sorry . . . ." Aunt Ella laughs. "Not a problem my child, but if memory serves me correctly, haven't you told me about your evening already."

"No, I don't mean with Jimmy, I mean earlier in the evening."

"Oh okay, well lets here it."

"Do you remember the man that came around yesterday?"

"The one who came looking for you?"

"Yes that very same one."

"So tell me all about the handsome young man."

"Well he came back last night and guess what happened."

"My dear, do I really want to know what happened."

"No, Aunt Ella, nothing like that." Aunt Ella mumbles to herself: "Well with the young men of today you can never be to sure."

"Sorry did you say something Aunt Ella?"

"No my dear, just tell me what happened."

"Well the handsome gentleman that you are referring to is Mr Blake and he just happens to be my new employer. He came here to inform me personally that my application was successful." Aunt Ella is looking at Abby with eyes filled with disbelief. "That's wonderful news, I'm so happy for you." She leans over and gives Abby a hug.

Aunt Ella looks Abby straight in the eyes, takes her hands and says: "See my child, all we need to do it put our faith and trust in the Lord and he will provide for his children. In Hebrew 13 the Lord says: "I will never leave thee nor forsake thee." That my dear is a promise from God, and you never have to doubt Gods promises. Somebody once said, If God brings you to the edge of a cliff you have to let go and fully trust in him. If you fall one of two things will happen. He will either catch you or teach you how to fly."

Abby was still thinking about the words that Aunt Ella had said long after she had left. The Lord has brought her to the edge of a cliff with the accident but she is not sure if he caught her or taught her how to fly.

Something tells her that he didn't do either, She feels like she is still standing at the edge of the cliff. The Lord needs her to let go and trust him to make the right choice. Until she has made peace with the accident and accepted the fact. She will never be able to move on and the Lord will never be able to show her the way.

She just can't, How can she let go of the thing that meant most to her if life, How can she let go without even saying a last goodbye. She thinks back on her parents. Her father was a Station-Master and her mother a housewife. They were the happiest people she had ever met.

They loved each other unconditionally. Abby always knew that one day when she got married she would want the same marriage as the one that her parents shared. She never heard them shout, scream, cuss or intentionally hurt one another. They always made decisions together and never got angry when it didn't work out as planned.

They saw it as a life's lesson. If one of them were sick the other would shower them with love and nurse them back to health. They always considered each other's needs. Abby wipes her tears and goes back into the apartment. She checks on Jimmy playing quietly on the bed with his cars. He notices her standing in the door way. "Hi Abby look my nose isn't bweeding anymore."

"I'm so happy to hear that." She walks to him and gives him a hug.

"Lets get you dressed, I's Saturday which means it our day to go to the park." Jimmy is ecstatic and shouts: "Jippy, we awe goin to the pawk."

Abby gets up and goes to the kitchen to prepare breakfast. A while later after they have eaten, she cleans the kitchen and they make their way to the park. Aunt Ella leant Abby her crutches to use in the mean time but luckily the part is just behind the block of flats so she doesn't have to walk very far.

Sally tells Jimmy about her new job on the way to the park and explains to him that he is still going to stay with Aunt Ella during the day. Jimmy is very excited when Abby explains to him that she will also now be able to afford sweets for him which she wasn't able to do before. He claps hands from excitement. Abby lays out the blanket on the grass for them to sit on in the park.

Aunt Ella packed them a small snack in a picnic basket. Jimmy goes off to play while Abby unpacks the picnic basket. She wants to warn him not to be to ruff because he is not feeling well but before she could she sees Jimmy is on his way back to her. "What's wrong why are you back so soon?"

"I don't want to play anymor I'm tiwed."

"Jimmy, you can't be tired already you only woke up about 4 hours ago. Come let's play with the ball."

"No, I don't wanna play wif the ball. I'm tiwed."

"So what do you want to do then?"

"I want you to read me a story."

"But Jimmy I didn't bring a book with to read to you."

"Then tell me a story."

Jimmy lies down with his head on her lap and she begins telling him a story. Half way through the story Abby realises that Jimmy is fast asleep. How is it possible that he could be sleeping again?

Maybe it's the medication that is making him drowsy e fact that her had very little sleep the night before. She will have to give the doctor a call on Monday to find out if any of the medication should have this effect on Jimmy.

She tries to wake him. "Jimmy, Jimmy its wake up time, you can't sleep now." Jimmy groans softly and opens his eyes. "I want to sleep; I'm tired when are we going home?"

"We can't go home we just got here and we haven't even touched the food in the picnic basket yet."

"But I want to go home."

"Oh Jimmy stop being so miserable." Jimmy starts throwing a tantrum; Abby gets upset and packs up the goodies.

"Ok Jimmy have it your way, let's go." Abby and Jimmy make their way home.

Chapter 8

"Have you heard a word I've said?" Cal looks at the man in front of him and says: "Sorry my friend, I'm not very good company today."

"I see so, what's her name?"

"Who's name?"

"The women that's got you on another planet." Cal looks at his best friend and frowns. "What makes you think it's a women?" Mark laughs softly and says: "There aren't any problems at the office otherwise you would have said something; the only other possible explanation is it has to be women. You forget we shared a dorm room for more than 5 years, sometimes I think I know you better than you know yourself. I can remember clearly the last time I saw you like this, but let's leave the past where it belongs. Tell me something about her, is she pretty, you never did like blondes?" Cal swallows the last sip of brandy in his glass and calls the waiter for a refill and says: "Another round please."

He waits for the waiter to bring the drinks before he starts talking: "You're right; it is a women, and a very pretty one at that. However she is complicated. The whole situation is complicated." Mark tilts his head and asks: "How complicated?" Cal grins. "Very complicated my friend, very complicated." Mark is very interested. "Do tell, maybe I can help. I'm all ears." Cal hesitates at first, but then he tells Mark everything from the Interview all the way to the last kiss. Mark leans back in his chair and listens attentively. When Cal finished telling him everything he runs his fingers through his hair and sighs deeply.

"I don't see why it has to be so complicated, you know what you have to do, so do it, tell her it was a mistake and it will never happen again."

"I can't get her out of my mind, just the fact that she has a boyfriend should already put me off, but it doesn't. In fact it makes me want her even more."

Mark sitting up straight in his chair shakes his head in disbelief. "You know how it feels to have someone be unfaithful to you. It's not something you would wish on your worst enemy. You will have to forget about her." Cal pulls himself together and says: "You are right my friend, I must forget about her. Come what may.

It's going to be more difficult than you think; I have just given her a job as my junior typist."

"You did what?"

"Oh you heard what I said."

"Well you can't go and tell her now that you made a mistake and she can't have the job. You are both adults and you will have to work it out."

"You are right, First thing Tuesday morning; I'll call her in and tell her were things standing and how it's going to work from now on."

Chapter 9

It's Tuesday morning, Abby walks nervously into her new job, and she had such night mares last night about the spiders. She will just have to be extra careful not to bump into one of them again. Luckily she put a can of insect replant in her hand bag this morning just in case she has another encounter with one of them.

She doesn't care whose collection they are. She will show no mercy if she finds one of them or one of their family members. This morning Abby is dressed in a light rose slack suite with white stripes that Sally gave her along with a few other designer label outfits as a present, when she visited yesterday.

When Sally gave her the present she was completely surprised. "It's' a small gift from me to you to make you look breath taking on your first day." Abby took the presents from Sally and opened them one by one. Abby is so grateful. "Oh Sally, you shouldn't have, it's too much. It must have cost a fortune."

"Oh stop complaining and try it on. I can't wait to see how it looks." Abby thanks Sally again for the present and starts to fit them on. Sally flattered Abby the whole evening till she left. "The clothes complement your figure." Abby must agree they do look good on her.

She really like the clothes Sally brought her but the shoes are similar to the ones she fell with, she refused to wear them. Abby goes straight to the reception desk and signs in.

Irene with a friendly smile, greets Abby. "Morning Miss Spence, and welcome to Blake Attorneys. I hope you will enjoy working here." Abby smiles kindly back. "Good morning to you to Mrs . . . ."

"Irene Grey, but just call me Irene"

"My name is Abby"

"Well then, it's a great pleasure to meet you, Abby."

The two woman smile at each other, as Irene says: "Let me take you to your new office and get you settle in. You are must be very excited." Abby smiles, but she is not really excited. She feels kind of awkward to see Mr Blake again. The last time after he kissed her, he just disappeared. Abby decides to act as normal as possible. She hopes he will spare her any kind of humiliation.

They reached the elevator, and Irene hit the button to open the door. While waiting for the elevator, Abby turns around and looks at all the people in the reception area. Is it possible that all these people are working in this building? Some of them must be visitors.

They look like ants gathering food for the winter. The elevator makes a sound when the doors opens, and Abby lets go of all her thoughts. She turned to enter the elevator, and the next moment she walks straight into someone. She lost her balance and just before she could hit the floor the person caught her. Abby blushes and apologizes.

The man smile at her when he speaks. "It's really me who should be apologizing. I was so engrossed in my own mind that I was not watching where I'm going." Abby smiles back. "No it's not your mistake, I turned so hastily without any warning."

"Well it seems to me we're both guilty for not watching where we were going."

Abby hesitates but then she says: "Thank you for breaking my fall, if not for you it would have been in front of everyone."

"Imagine what excitement it would have been for them." Says the man with laugher in his eyes. Abby is actually supposed to be angry at the man who thinks it might be exciting to see someone fall, but his face is very open and sincere. She could see in his eyes he tried to dismiss it as a joke. Instead she says. "Well thanks to you, there will be no excitement for them." They both laugh. "I'm glad you caught me in time."

"The gratification is mine." Then the man stretched out his hand and introduces himself to her. "Where are my manners, my name is Mark." Abby takes his hand and say: "My name is Abby." From the elevator Irene calls Abby. "Hey Abby your boss is waiting for you." She let go of the man's hand and walked into the elevator.

Mark's waving hand is the only thing she sees before the doors close. There is silence in the elevator all the way to the top. The doors open and Abby follows Irene into the corridor. As they are walking towards the door, Abby's confidence starts fading with every step that she takes. How will she be able to work with a man that she can't resist?

She slows down for a moment and takes a deep breath. They reach the door that leads into the sixth storey. "Well here we are. Come right this way." And Irene directs her in the way of Mr Blake's office. Cal's attention is captivated in the papers before him. He doesn't even notice when the two women enter his office. Only when Irene stand in front of his desk and tapped her finger on the table he became aware of them. Cal hears the ticking and then looks up with an annoyance in his eyes.

Then he looked past the woman before him to the woman behind her. She looks breath-taking this morning. The slack suit that she is wearing, compliment each curve. Her hair is a bush of black tresses and hanging over her shoulders. Abby feels his eyes on her and she looks at him across the room.

Their dark brown and bright green eyes meet. They forget about the other woman in the office. Abby heart beats faster end she tries to look away, but without any success. He looks incredibly handsome in his black suit. The baby blue tie that he is wearing, compliments his eyes in a strange yet dazzling way. Cal remembers what Mark said and he breaks eye contact with Abby.

Irene breaks the silence when she says: "Good morning Mr. Blake, I brought your typist. Would you like me to show her around, or would you prefer to do it yourself?" Cal didn't actually pay attention to what Irene said. All he can think about is the woman with the black curls. He knows he must talk to her about what happened.

He must inform her that it was a mistake and it won't happen again. You know she is involved with someone else and she is forbidden to you. From now on it's only going to be professional relationship between the two of them. It's going to be hard to do it, but it must be done. They need to get the record as straight as the crow flies. He rises from his chair and looks at Irene who is still waiting for him to answer her. With rage he gathers his feelings together, and tries to get a hold of himself. "Thank you Irene for bringing Mrs Spence, I'll take it from here." Irene greets him and then she turns to Abby, smiles and greets her kindly before she disappears out of the door.

Cal comes to stand before Abby. He puts on an act and say: "Good morning Mrs Spence. How is your foot feeling?"

"Good morning Mr Blake. My foot has heeled remarkably." Cal doesn't really know what to say anymore, so he turns around and take his seat again. With his hand he directs Abby to take a seat on one of the leather chairs. He looks her directly in the eyes and say: "Mrs Spence before we commence there are some things that we need to straighten out."

He waits for a while and then continues. "What happened between us . . . . ? It was my mistake, and I am apologetic for my actions. I can guarantee you; it will under no circumstances happen again." A feeling of tribulation fills Abby's heart. She has no idea where it came from or why she is feeling this way.

Cal looks at Abby and sees regret in her eyes. Does she regret kissing him? Maybe she feels she has betrayed her special person. Just the thought of other man in her life makes him grind on his teeth.

He realizes he is being unreasonable, so he gets control over himself. He manages to be in charge of the discussion which is still up in the air. He looks down at his hands that are spread out wide on the table. With his eyes on his hands, the reminiscences of them holding her in his arms, is embossed in his brain. You've come so far, so you might as well draw to a close. He says to himself. Cal hoists up his head and say: "I hope we are on the same page." Abby not in a condition to say anything, just knots her head.

Cal sees it and at that moment he gathers all his courage and move to the next area under discussion. "I am delighted that we both agree on that subject." It's all been said, but Cal is not content. He didn't like Abby saying nothing, nor the impression on her face of not being bothered by the fact that they will only be employer and employee. Well, thinks Cal to himself. If it doesn't bother her, it won't bother me. Cal regains control of himself, looks her straight in the eye and says: "Now that we both agree to that matter, we can get to business. The position you applied for, contains more than what the advert portrayed.

Your duties won't only be typing, but it will also include this." And Cal hands her a sheet of paper with all the other duties explained. Abby takes the paper that he hands her, and rapidly goes through it. Then she looks back at him and say: "Doesn't look like rocket science, I'm sure there will be no problem."

"Good to hear. Your office is temporarily in construction, so for time being you will be working in my office. I'll arrange for a desk and a computer to be brought to my office as soon as possible." At the drop of a hat, Cal picks up the phone and dials a number. Soon she hears him demanding a desk and computer to his office over the phone.

After he is satisfied he hangs up. "The desk and computer will be here in approximately two hours. There are a number of letters that need to be typed, so you can use my laptop while waiting." Cal gets on his feet and shows Abby to come and sit down in his chair. A nervous Abby rises from her chair and moves around the table towards his chair. She takes a seat, but soon realizes she has got to sit on the edge of the chair to be able to reach the laptop. Cal notice what she is doing, and adjusts the seat for her so she can sit comfortable.

Abby thanks him and then he shows her the pile of letters which must be typed. "I'll be leaving shortly for a meeting that I must attend. Before I go, I need to warn you to keep that door closed at all times." Cal points at the door in the wall. "We sure don't want a repeat of what happened the other day."

Abby looks at him with perplexity on her face. "The spider family lives there." At first Abby got frighten, but then she remembers the can of insect replant in her bag, and smiles at him. "Don't worry about that. I've got everything under control." It's Cal turn to be confused now. "Just about four days ago you were terrified of the spiders and all of a sudden you have everything under control? What's up with the change?"

"Oh noooo . . . . There is . . . noo change . . . , it's just that . . . . if I keep the door closed, like you suggested . . . I'll be fine." Abby realizes this man can't be fooled. Sooner or later he will find out about the can of insect replant. She wishes he would just leave. Then he turns around and leaves the office. Abby stares at him while he is walking out the door. When he close the door behind him, Abby heaves a sigh out loud.

Abby is so captivated in her work that she doesn't even notice the two men who are bringing the desk and computer in to the office. Only when one of the two men spoke to her, she became aware that she is not alone. "Where would you like us to put it down?" Abby's not sure and leaves it to the two men to find an appropriated place for it.

They choose, however, one corner of the office that is vacant. After a while the two men are finished. They turn to Abby and ask her if she is satisfied. She just lifts her head and nod's. The two men leave the office and once again Abby is alone. She takes another pile of letters and starts typing again.

Abby gets frighten when someone places a hand on her shoulder. "Hi sorry didn't mean to fright you." Abby looks up into a pair of bright blue eyes. She has never seen this woman before. She is very good-looking, with long blond hair that flows beyond her shoulders.

She looks like one of those ladies who are normally used on cosmetic advertisements. Her attire testifies a wealthy background. Abby tries to estimate how old the lady next to her is. She looks very young though, but then again with the latest cosmetic creams available, it's not easy to determine how old women really are. She dares not to ask. Abby know that she shouldn't been judging a book by its cover, but there is something about this lady that gives Abby the creeps. She reminds Abby of the characters in the fairytales her parents use to read to her and her sister. It's not the fairies which this lady reminds Abby about, but the evil wicked witches.

Suddenly Abby gets Goosebumps by just the thought. The lady's shrill voice brings Abby back to reality. "I just wanted to come and see how it's going. I've heard Kate has been replaced, so I wanted to get acquainted. My name is Leonie Coater, and she extends her hand to Abby. At first Abby doesn't take her hand, but then her good manners get a hold of her. She puts her hand into Leonie's hand and shakes it. "And I am . . . ."

"Abby Spence. I know."

"You know?"

"Of course, everybody knows about Cal's new typist. You're the news of the day."

"Oh I see."

"You know, I don't want to gossip . . . . Consider this as a friendly warning." Leonie takes a seat in one of the leather chairs and proceed. "You must be wary of Cal. He has the reputation of a federal dog when it comes to women. In fact, it's the reason why his wife walked out on him." Abby is quit shocked but tries not to show it.

She didn't know he was married. She wonders if he has any children, but refuses to ask. He made it clear this morning that they are only employer and employee, so his personal life has got nothing to do with her. Just the thought of it makes her feel sick. She wishes this evil wickedness could just disappear. Abby had enough for one day. She looks Leonie straight in the eye and says: "Mr Blake's personal life has got nothing to do with me. I am only an employee, and I intend to keep it that way. Now if you would excuse me please, these letters needs to be typed before Mr Blake arrives back at the office. She points with her finger to the pile of written letters." Leonie gets up from her chair and gives Abby a loftily look before she walks out the door without saying good bye. Abby take the last few letters and start typing again. For two hours she works very hard to get all the letters done in time. After a while Abby peaks at her wrist watch and see it is almost time to go home. Luckily she finished all the letters. Abby takes a sheet of paper and makes a cover, then she places the pile of typed letters into the cover and puts it on a spot where Mr Blake can see it. She turns to the laptop and switches it off. She looks around the office to see if everything is neat and tidy, only then she gets her bag en walk out the office.

Abby fills the bathtub with water. She puts her hand in the water to feel the temperature. She walks towards the bathroom door and calls Jimmy. "Jimmy! Jimmy!" he came from out the bedroom and says: "I donna wanna bawf."

"Jimmy you must bath."

"No . . . I wanna pay some mor."

"I tell you what. Why don't you get in the tub, and I'll fetch you some toys to play with." Jimmy looks like he is considering Abby's offer. Then he slowly starts taking off his clothes. Abby is very relieved with the boy's decision, and takes off to the bedroom to get his toys. With the toys in her hands she walks towards the bathroom. Jimmy already got in the tub and is waiting patiently for his toys. Abby hands him a dinosaur, boat and a few cars. He accepts the toys and start playing with them. Abby leaves him to play for a while and goes to the kitchen to prepare supper.

Abby is almost done with supper when Jimmy calls. "Abby I'm finies paying !"

"Just a moment I'll be with you now." She finishes the supper and walks to the bedroom to get Jimmy's pyjamas and then to the bathroom. "Stand up so that I can wash you. Jimmy gets up, Abby takes the soap and starts washing him. She first washes the front of his body and then his feet. Then she tells him to turn around so that she can wash his back. Jimmy turns around and Abby see a blue patch on his back. She scowls and asks him: "Jimmy how did you manage to get such a big blue patch on your back?" Jimmy shakes his head. "I don now."

"You must be more careful my boy."

Chapter 10

This past week Abby has learned a lot from her new job. Although it is very exhaustive, she enjoyed every moment of it. In time she had also moved to her own desk. Mr Blake was mostly out of the office, but it didn't bother her, because it gave her a chance to get used to her new environment.

Some of the other employees have come and introduced themselves, and also offered assistance if she would need something. She is still struggling to become accustomed to the spider family on the other side of the wall. Even though Mr Blake ensured her they are safe in their tank, she cannot stop thinking about that day that the spider sat on her hand. Luckily she hasn't run into one of the spiders family members recently.

She held the door shut and locked as Mr Blake commanded her, but frequently found herself looking around most of the time searching for one of them on the floor. The can of insect replant is still in her bag and ready to be used if necessary. With the thought that she has some kind of protection she is ready to begin the day. Abby picks up the paper which Mr Black writes all the duties for the day that needs to get done. She takes a seat at her desk and starts reading trough his instructions. There is not much to do for today. Mr Blake is attending meetings this morning so he will only be back after lunch. Abby starts to complete her duties flawlessly one by one. After tea she has accomplished more than she expected she would. Irene came by to see if she could be of any assistance. Abby assured her she had everything under control. Abby sits in her chair, and she is very tired. She thinks about last night. Jimmy's nose bled twice and again he had a fever. It was one of those nights which neither Abby nor Jimmy got any sleep. She did phone the doctor this morning but he was unavailable, and she left a message for him to call her back. Abby leans back in her chair and for a moment she closes her eyes.

The meeting went better than he expected. Everyone was happy with his decisions. A very satisfied Cal gets into his car and starts the engine. He puts the car into gear and pulls away. He can't wait to get to the office. He has been thinking a lot about Abby. The past week he forced himself not to go to the office, because with Abby in the vicinity it's difficult to get any work done. The few times he had to go to the office he caught himself staring at her and thinking about the day he kissed her in that very same office. Many times he felt like doing it again, but he controls himself. He kept thinking about her special person, and it makes his blood boil. Just the thought of another man who has the privilege to kiss her when he feels like it, awakes the green eyed monster inside Cal. He accelerates and skips a red robot. He can't wait to get to the office. All he wants to do now is look at her. Even though it will be from across the room. He reaches the underground parking of the big old grey building. He slows down and parks his car. Cal gets out of his car and walk straight towards the elevator. When the doors open, he walks in and hit the number 6 button. The journey to the sixth floor feels like an eternity. At last he reaches the sixth floor and the doors finally open. He walks out into the corridor straight to his office. While walking a strange feeling gets hold of him, but he pushes it aside. He can't wait to see her again. He opens the office door and walks in. He looks at her and rigid in his tracks. The picture that he sees is not exactly what he expected. She sits in her chair, and she is sleeping. His first instinct is to go wake her with a kiss. He moves closer to her. He looks down at her face, and can't resist stroking her check. She is in motion by the touch of his hand. Cal thinks to himself. She is even lovelier when she sleeps. Her lips are slightly apart, and Cal has no power over himself. He lowers his head. At first he just stokes his lips against hers, and before he could kiss her, Mark's words appears in his conscience mind. "She is involved with someone else." It makes him lift his head again and takes a step backwards. He is angry with himself for being so weak when it comes to this woman. He looks at her again and wonders why she is sleeping when she is supposed to working. Suddenly a thought appears in his mind. Maybe she and her special person had a late night. Anger and jealousy makes him hit hard with his hand on Abby's desk. Abby wakes up and look into a furious face. She realizes she must've been sleeping. Quickly she sits up straight in her chair. "I'm sorry . . . . I didn't mean to . . . ." Something in Cal eyes forces her to remain silent. Cal grates the words out angrily: "Miss Spence, I pay you to work not to sleep." Abby thinks of something to say, but her courage engages her. He leans a little forward and says with horror in his voice. "If you don't get enough sleep through the night due to a late night with your special person, then it's your problem, but don't let it interfere with your job." Abby is now also filled with anger and thinks to herself. This unscrupulous buffalo, I bet he never had to spend a whole night with a sick child. Cal sees the anger in her eyes and he takes a step closer to her. He lifts her chin with his thumb and asked: "Tell me Miss Spence, does your special person kiss better than me?" Abby stares at him with total confusion. For a moment she has no idea what or who the special person is that he repeatedly refers to. Then she remembers the night he came to her apartment, and the bedroom door she closed. She said that her special person was sleeping and that she didn't want to wake him. She actually referred to Jimmy when she said her special person, but he doesn't know it. This man must have made his own conclusions and thought she was talking about a boyfriend or something. Well if that's what's he is thinking, so be it. Abby decides to leave him in the dark; he doesn't deserve to know the truth after being so rude to her. A smile ripple around her mouth and Cal notices it. With admiration in her eyes she says to him. "Better, Mr Blake, much better. In fact you could learn a lot from him." The next moment Cal pulls her out of her chair and puts his lips hard on her lips. The kiss is filled with anger and frustration. He is mad at her, because she prefers another man rather than him. After a while he lets her go. Abby is so off balance that she has to hold on to the desk for support. With a livid face she looks at him, but he doesn't even notice it. All he does is look her straight in the eye and says: "Don't ever challenge me again, unless you want me to loose all my self control." He turns around and storms out of the office.

Long after Cal left Abby still has not recovered from what happened. She tries to make sense out of his last words, and before she could come to a conclusion, the phone rings. She picks it up to answer. "Mr Blake's office, Abby speaking how may I assist you?"

"Miss Spence please."

"Oh, it is her speaking."

"Good day Miss Spence. It's Doctor Grey speaking. I got a message to phone you back."

"Yes Doctor . . . thanks for returning my call." Abby first hesitates and then she speaks. "I called you in connection with Jimmy."

"What seems to be the problem Miss?"

"Well . . . . Doctor, I'm a little worried about him. With his last visit, Doctor prescribed an antibiotic for throat infection, which should be completed over ten days. He has hitherto completed the course, but I can't see any sign of improvement. He still complains about a sore throat, and is constantly feverish."

"That is a bit strange. Why don't you bring him in tomorrow so I can examine him again? Let me just confirm with the receptionist what time is available. Please hold the line." After a while she hears the doctor's voice again.

"Miss Spence?"

"Yes Doctor?"

"Would nine o'clock suit you?"

"Yes, thank you Doctor."

"Well . . . till tomorrow then. Have a good day Miss Spence."

"You too Doctor." She hangs up the phone. Abby looks at the pile of papers that needs to be filed. She pick's it up carefully and walk towards the filing cabinet. Abby starts filing the papers. At last she is finished and she looks at her wrist watch to see what time it is. With shock she sees it is almost seven o'clock. Abby walks towards her desk and switch off the computer. She grabs her bag and leaves the office. Abby turns to lock the office door when she hears voices. For a moment she thought she had imagined it, but then it gets increasingly clear. She stood still, and it sounds like two people quarrelling. If she is not mistaking, the voices come from the office next door. Abby moves closer to the office and not only can she hear the voices loud and clear, she can also identify them. The one voice belongs to Mr Blake there's no doubt about that, and the other voice belongs to Leonie. Abby recognised her voice because of the shrillness in it. Then she hears Cal's voice again and he sounds very disgruntled about something. Leonie cries while she is speaking. "What am I suppose to do Cal? I can't do this on my own. You must help me. It's not my child alone." Then Cal says impatiently: "I'm sorry Leonie I can't help you, you are on your own." Abby suddenly feels sick. She moves as quickly as possible into the corridor. She makes her way to the elevator, and is very thankful the doors are open. Abby hit the button and the doors close. While she is moving down, she thinks about what she had just herd. Abby can't believe what her boss told the other woman. The elevator doors opens and Abby flew through the reception area towards the main entrance. Outside the building she takes a deep breath and walks in the direction of the bus stop.

Abby rings Aunt Ella's doorbell. After a few seconds Aunt Ella opens the door. With friendliness she greets Abby and invites her in. Abby walks past Aunt Ella to the living room. She looks down at Jimmy were he is playing with his toys. "Hello my sweat heart." Jimmy looks up to Abby and his eyes sparkles when he greets her back. "Hello Abby." Then he gets up from the floor and walks to her with his arms in the air. Abby pick's him up and they hug each other. "How was your day?"

"Nice." With the boy still in her arms, she takes a seat. "What did you do today?" Jimmy tells Abby about everything he and Aunt Ella did during the day. He tells her about the dog they saw when they went for a walk and he tells her about the cake they had baked. Abby stares at Jimmy while he tells her about the day's proceedings. Although he tells his story very excitedly, she notices that he is not healthy. The next moment Jimmy's nose starts to bleed. Aunt Ella, who was busy making tea, rushes her to the bathroom to get some tissues. She comes back with a box full and hands it over to Abby. Jimmy knows to bend over and to breathe trough his mouth while Abby put some pressure on his nose. While they are waiting for Jimmy's nose to stop bleeding, Abby looks over the boy's head straight into Aunt Ella's face which is filled with fear. Aunt Ella takes a seat on the chair closest to her and asks Abby: "Why is his nose bleeding dear?" Abby sighs and shakes her head. "I don't know. I spoke to the doctor this afternoon, and he said I must bring

Jimmy in tomorrow so that he can examine him again. I'll ask Sally if she is available to take us, because she normally visits her parents on weekends."

Abby and Jimmy are waiting for the doctor's in his consulting room. Abby looks down at Jimmy and sees that he looks kind of nervous. She leans over to his side and gives him a hug. He looks back at her and she smiles at him. Then the doctor makes his appearance. Abby gets up from her seat and greets the doctor as friendly as he greeted her. He walks around the desk and takes his seat. He opens a file and looks Abby straight in the eye. "Miss Spence yesterday when we spoke over the phone, you mentioned that you are worried because there seems to be no improvement regarding Jimmy? I must agree with you on that term. You also mentioned that he is constant feverish and he still complains about the sore throat?"

"Yes Doctor, and the past few days, his nose would just start bleeding for no reason." Doctor Grey thinks for a moment and then he speaks. "Miss Spence I think we should draw some blood. I'll send a blood sample to the lab and they will be able to determine what is wrong with him. It normally takes two to three days for the results to get back. As soon as we know what the results are, we can take it from there." Abby nods her head and says: "If this is the only way we will determine what is wrong with him, then we have to do it." Abby then turns to Jimmy and say: "Sweat heart comes let's go sit on the bed." She takes his hand and leads him towards the bed. First she makes sure his is comfortable before she takes a seat next to him. Abby takes his little hand into her own and tries to explain to him what's going to happen now. "Jimmy the doctor is going to draw some blood from your arm. Is that okay with you?" Jimmy nods his head and Abby smiles at the little boy's bravery. The doctor comes closer to them with the needle. As much as Abby tries to draw Jimmy's attention away from the needle, the more she fails. His eyes are fixed on the needle. The needle goes into Jimmy's arm, and Abby can see the tears rolling down his cheeks and she reaches over to wipe it off with the back of her thumb. Then the needle gets exchanged for cotton. Abby helps Jimmy climb off the bed, with his hand still in hers. Doctor Grey opens the drawer of his desk and takes out two lollipops. He walks towards Jimmy and bends down to look Jimmy in the eyes and asks him: "Are you angry with me?"

"No." The doctor strokes Jimmy hair and hands him the two lollipops. "Fank you doker."

"Pleasure is mine."

The doctor rises and greets Abby with a friendly smiles. "Enjoy the rest of your day, and I'll get back to you as soon as the results are back from the lab."

"Thank you Doctor, and do enjoy your day as well." Then Abby and Jimmy leave the consulting room and walk straight to Sally who has been waiting for them the whole time in the waiting room.

Chapter 11

Wednesday morning Abby walks into the office dog-tired as usually. She is so relieved that it's Wednesday, because today Jimmy's test results are coming back from the lab. Now that the doctor can determine what's wrong with Jimmy, he can prescribe the right medication that would heal Jimmy. The last few days she had some trouble keeping up with Jimmy. He nose were bleeding again, his throat stays sore and then there is the fever that won't subside.

Her thoughts comes to and end when Cal enters the office. He walks striate towards her and stops in front of her desk. For a moment he just looks at her and then he begins to speak: "Miss Spence you must go to the Human Recourse's department on the second floor. Jenny is waiting for you." With that he turns around and take a seat at his own desk. Abby gets up from her chair and walks out the office.

Cal stares at her until she closes the door behind her. Ever since he kissed her on Friday, he could stop thinking about her. She remains in his thoughts. Over the weekend Mark and Cal got together for a round of golf. It was hard to concentrate on the game. All he wanted to do was to go to Abby. Mark must have noticed something was bugging him, because he mentioned Abby.

Cal tried his best to deny it, but Mark couldn't be fooled. He could see that Cal is head over heels. This shocked Cal and kept him wondering the whole time until now. He's not in love with her, it's only lust that she awakes in him. He was in love once before, and it turned out not quite as he planed. Amanda's beauty swept him off his feet. He was blindly in love with her and was prepared to move heaven and earth to keep her happy. Unfortunately it wasn't enough for her. Amanda soon got a other guy and she filled for a divorce. Cal was devastated by her betrayal, and let her have her way. He promised himself, after what happened to him with Elisabeth's rejection and Amanda's betrayal, he would never trust a woman again. he refuses to let them into his live.

A knock on the door brings Cal back to reality. "Come in!" A very thin man with a bunch of red roses enters the office. He walks straight towards Cal and say: "The roses are for Miss Spence. The lady down at the reception referred me up here." Cal looks at the man and is very abrupt when he speak. "Miss Spence is currently busy, just put the roses on her desk."

"I would need you to sign this." The man holds a paper out to him. Cal takes it and sign, then he returns it to the man. The delivery man greets Cal and walks out the door. Cal is very upset about the roses. He doesn't need to guess who the sender are, he knows. It's her special person who sent it to her.

Abby returns to the office. She is hardly trough the door when she sees Cal standing with a bunch of red roses at her desk. He looks up at sees Abby walking towards him. Then he hands her the bunch of roses and say: "These for you." Abby looks at the roses and answers sarcastically." Thank you for the gesture, but red is not really my colour." Cal seems surprised at her remark. The thought hits him, she thinks he bought her the roses. With admiration in his eyes he leans forward whispers in her ears: "My dear, the roses you are referring to, are not from me. I will never give a woman roses especially not red ones. Do you want to know why? I'll tell you why, because when a lady sees red they tend to mistaken it for love, and I don't believe in love. The heart is there to circulate the blood to the brain to keep your body functioning." Cal takes her chin between his fingers and say: "I think that it may be from your special person. What I would like to know, is what he sinned, that it was necessary for him to sent you such an expensive bouquet? At first Abby was confused to hear that the bouquet is not from him, because there's no one else that could have sent her the roses. Now, Abby thinks back to what he said about her special person, and it makes her laughs. With a secretive look in her eyes, she moves closer to him and whispers in his ear, as he did to her. "In my eyes that special person whom you so often refer to, can do nothing wrong. In fact I forgive him before he has even done it. For your information, he doesn't have to buy me roses nor does he have to say he is sorry. Do you want to know why? Let me tell you why, I love him more than I love myself. The fact that you are jealous," Abby continuous with confidence. Flatters me, but there is no need for you to be jealous of Jimmy. I really can't see what threat a three year old boy can be to you." Cal stares at her with disbelief. He thinks he is hallucinating. Did he hear correctly? Is the her special person a little boy three years of age? He draws her closer to him and says: "You have made me the happiest man alive." He bends down to kiss her, then the phone rings. Abby untangles herself from his arms. She reaches for the phone and answers it. "Good morning, Mr Blake's office, Abby speaking. How may I assist you?"

"Good day, Miss Spence please."

"This is she."

"Miss Spence, it's Doctor Grey here. I've received the test results from the lab . . . . I need you to bring Jimmy in right away, because the prognosis doesn't look good at all."

Abby can't get a word out. It's feels like someone has ripped out her heart. With the phones still in her hand the tears role down her cheek. Cal sees how pale she has become and doesn't understand what's happening. Without saying goodbye she hangs up the phone. With a look of emptiness on her face she says to Cal: "I have to go."

"Where to? Why? What's happening?" Abby realizes she has got to tell him something. "That was Jimmy's doctor, he wants to see him immediately. The lab results came back and I need to go get him."

"Where is he?"

"At Aunt Ella's"

"Who is Aunt Ella?"

"She is my neighbour, the one you spoke to when you came looking for me."

"I'll just get my car keys and jacked than we can go."

"There's no need for you . . . ."

"I am taking you and I won't tolerate any objections." Abby just nods her head and grabs her bag. Together they make they way to the elevator. They are standing before the two iron doors of the elevator, waiting for it to open. Eventually the doors open, and they get in. The doors close and they make their way to the underground parking area. They exit the elevator and rush to the car. He open the passenger side for her and helps her get in before he gets behind the wheel. He starts the engine, puts the car in gear and pulls away.

Within minutes they reach Aunt Ella's apartment, and Cal turns off the engine. Abby rushes to the front door of Aunt Ella's apartment, with Cal following directly behind her. She enters the apartment without knocking. Abby finds an devastated Aunt Ella in the kitchen holding a apron against Jimmy's mouth. The little boy's facial expression tells Abby that he is terrified. Abby moves towards aunt Ella and Jimmy. She removes the apron from Jimmy's mouth and almost faints at the sight of all the blood pouring out of Jimmy's mouth. Abby now terrified herself, looks at Aunt Ella. "I phoned the office and they said you had left already. Then I phoned the doctor and he advised me you were on your way to come and get Jimmy's. What's wrong dear?"

"Aunt Ella I can't explain now, I need to get Jimmy to the doctor." Aunt Ella looks across the room, she notices Cal as he is walking towards Abby. They great each other briefly. Cal touches Abby's shoulder and says: "We need to get going." He picks Jimmy up from the counter and the little boy with a tear-stained face and big eyes stares up at him. Cal help's Abby in the direction of the door. Outside they move quickly to get in the car. Abby gets in the car while Cal lays Jimmy down on the back seat.

Cal drives faster than the speed of light. In less than no time, they reach the doctors consulting room. Cal parks the car and while Abby gets out, he opens the back door and picks Jimmy up. Cal is relieved to see that the bleeding has stopped. With Jimmy in Cal's arms and Abby close behind them, they enter the Doctor's rooms. Abby walks to the receptionist and identifies herself. The receptionist nods her head and pick's up the earpiece of the phone to inform the doctor of Jimmy's arrival. The doctor appears in the reception area and calls Abby into the consulting room. Just as Cal is about to follow Abby, a woman stops him. Jimmy seems to know the lady and Cal pauses in his footsteps. "Ant Hattie, my mouwf was weeding." Jimmy holds out his arms and Sally takes him.

"I know my Cheeck chop, Aunt Ella told me. She phoned me when you left." Cal introduces himself to Sally. "I am Cal Blake, Abby's boss."

"I am Sally, Abby's best friend. Under the circumstances It's a pleasure to meet you. Speaking of which, were is Abby?"

"She is the consulting room." Sally can see that Cal is aiming in that direction, and says: "It's okay, you can go if like, I'll keep Jimmy with me." Cal hesitates, but then he walks off. In the consulting room, Doctor Grey looks at both Abby and Cal very seriously and speaks. "What I'm about to tell you, might upset you, but it is imperative that you listen carefully." Doctor Grey takes a breath and continues. "Regarding our telephonic conversation, the results of Jimmy's blood tests have returned and the prognosis is not good. I'm regret to inform you that Jimmy is a victim of Acute Leukaemia. We will have to admit him immediately so that we can start treatment and if that does not succeed then we will make him as comfortable as possible." There is silence in the room, Abby is the one to break it: "How Long . . . . ?"

"We can never be sure but it looks like two months at the most."

"No it can't be."

"I'm afraid it is." Abby burst into tears and turns to Cal for comfort, which he willingly provides. "No. It can't be. No, no, no!" Abby is now on her feet. "Please doctor, there must be something you can do. I can't loose him to."

Dr Grey knows exactly what she is talking about because he is the one that gave her the injection the night of the accident. Cal thinks to himself, Clearly, she had lost someone close to her not long ago, but who he wonders. Could it be the boys father? There is no time to ponder over this now, Abby is all that matter at the moment. Abby and Jimmy. He takes her hands into his and says:" Abby, I'm sure the doctors will do everything they possibly can and won't give up until they do." Let me take you home so that you can pack a bag for Jimmy." Abby shakes her head. "No, I'm going with him to the hospital he is to young and he won't understand what is happening to him and why." Cal looks at the doctor and asks:" What is the name of the hospital you are taking him to?" The doctor provides him with the name of a government hospital.

Cal turns to Abby and says:" Go make arrangements with Sally to pack Jimmy a bag, I'll join you in a few minutes." He opens the door and pushes her gently into the hall way. Abby walks toward the waiting room and there she finds Sally and Jimmy. Jimmy is the first one to see her and calls out to her:" Abby, wook Aunt Hatty is hewre."

"I see that yes." Sally looks up at Abby with questionable eyes:" What's wrong?" The only word Abby can get out is the name of the virus, which infected Jimmy's whole body. Cal returns to the waiting room, He stood still a while, watching the scene before him. The first thought that hit him was that he was wrong about Abby. Everything he suspected her of, let him feel ashamed. Today he met the real Abby Spence. She is a loving mother that would do everything in her power, to take away all the hurt and pain. He thinks back to his mother, if he was that sick would Elizabeth have stayed with him? Cal feels the tears which is trending to come out, and takes a deep breath. He know the answer to that question. She wouldn't have. She would have never sacrificed her happiness for him, in fact he was the one who ended up doing the sacrificing.

Chapter 12

Jimmy sits on the hospital bed, and watches everything around him. It's only the toy cars his holding in his hands, which are familiar. He looks with big eyes at the door. Abby said she is going to buy him some ice-cream and sweets, but she is taking so long. The tears form droplets on his cheeks. Jimmy wonders to himself. Why am I hewe? Everybody is wearing white clothes. Gramps always said in heaven people are wearing white. Maybe he is in heaven. His eyes stretch wide. He can visit Aunt Ella's daughter. Fist he must find Jesus to ask him if he can take her home to Aunt Ella, cause she misses her a lot. With the idée he climbs off the bed and walks cautiously towards the door. In the passage he sees Sally, and he troughs his hands in the air. Sally smiles at him and pick him up. "Hey you must be in bed, why are you walking around? By the way where is Abs?"

"She went to buy me sweets and ice-cweam."

"Your teeth will rot if you eat to many sweets."

"Nooo."

"Is."

"Nooo."

"Sally stop teasing him." Abby stands behind Sally. Both Jimmy and Sally turn their heads to look at Abby.

"I'm not teasing him, I'm just saying that his teeth will rot."

"Nooo, it will not."

"Well if you eat to many sweets it will." Abby causes interference. "As long as you brush your teeth, it shouldn't rot." Jimmy looks at Sally triumphantly, and Sally pulls a face. Then all of a sudden Sally remembers about the gift she brought jimmy. "I'll be back soon." Abby takes his hands in hers and asks: "How are you feeling?"

"Goowd . . . . am I in heawven?" Abby is shocked with Jimmy's question. "What makes you ask such a thing?"

"Gramps aways saiwd people in heawven awl wewre white." Abby looks sadly towards Jimmy. Sally comes into the room with a teddy bear almost twice Jimmy's length. Jimmy's eyes open wide when he sees it. Sally smiled broadly and handed the toy to Jimmy. "You must take good care of him and watch over him, Okay?"

"Yes Awnty Hatty, I will I pwomise. Thank you." She walks closer to him and gives him a hug." It's a pleasure my Cheeky Chop." She looked at her wristwatch and says:" Oh look at the time, I have to go but I'll see you soon." She went over to Abby and kissed her on the cheek she then gave Jimmy a kiss on the cheek to. She disappeared out the door.

Jimmy lays in the bed and Abby pages through a magazine. She hears someone knocking softly on the door and looks up. Cal came in the room and walked straight over to her. He bent down and kissed her on the cheek. He looked her in the eyes and asked:" How is he doing?" Abby looks at Jimmy, he is fast asleep then looks up at Cal:" Under the circumstances I think it's going well. He's so small and innocent. It's unfair that such a young child should suffer such a traumatic disease. He still has his whole life ahead of him." Meanwhile Cal takes a seat next to Abby on the other chair. He thinks about what she has just said and looks at her. Saddened he says:" Sometimes life is unfair, unfortunately there is nothing we can do about it." Abby thinks about what Cal said. He is right life is not fair, but why should Jimmy be the one that life is being unfair towards? Why him?

There are so many questions in her head but she tries not to think about it. She turned to Cal, He has been so good to them. When the doctor told her that he was sending Jimmy to a private Medical Centre she had to protest. She said that a private Medical Centre would cost far to much for her.

The doctor told here not to worry, that provisions have been made for Jimmy to be cared for in a private medical centre. She wanted to know how or who was responsible for making this happen. At first the doctor wouldn't say and Abby begged and pleaded with him to tell her. Eventually the doctor gave in and told her that it was Cal Blake, her boss, that had made it possible for Jimmy to go. The first question she asked herself was, why would he do this?

This is the first time that she had seen him since Jimmy had been admitted to the hospital. Suddenly she realised that she had not yet thanked him:" Cal, I haven't had a chance to thank you for what you did, for Jimmy and myself. It was not necessary, I don't know how I will ever repay you, but I will make a plan. What I can't understand is why you would do it?"

Cal heard every word she said, he found himself asking that same question, why did I do it? The answer hit him, His heart screamed at him. It's because you love her you fool. Cal is surprised by the answer his heart told his head, however. He knows it's true. And he said it too: I did it because I love you." Abby stares at him, incredulously. "What?

You love me? Cal I thought you don't believe in love. You said so yourself."

He runs his hands through his hair and looks to the floor while saying:" It's because I have never experienced it. It's the first time in my life that I have felt this way about anyone, and it's you. I don't know how it happened, but it did."

He told her all about his childhood. He told her of his father, his mother, his stepfather and his failed marriage. He has never shared this with anyone, except for Mark. He doesn't know why he told her everything, but he feels he must. He trusts her with his deepest secret. He closes with." I love you Abby Spence and I want you to marry me." He lifted his head and looked at her. "Will you?" Abby's heart skips a beat or two, She can't believe what she has just heard. Did he really ask me to marry him? Did I hear him correctly? Before she could answer him she heard Jimmy's voice calling out to her.

She stood up from her seat and sat on the edge of the bed. "Yes honey, here I am. What's the matter?" Jimmy partially opens his eyes and looks at her. He tries to sit up straight but falls back. It breaks her heart to see him like this. She felt so helpless because she knows there is nothing she can do for him to help take the pain away. She put her hand on his, and feels the tears in the tear duct ready to come out. She felt Cal standing behind her so she leaded back against him for support.

He looked at Jimmy staring at them with a bunch of questions in his eyes. He looked very sick today. His face is pale. Cal spoke with the doctor this morning to get an update on the treatment progress, and how long they would still have Jimmy in there lives. The doctor advised him that Jimmy is not responding to any of the treatments. There are still a few option to consider, but he is not sure that it will help.

Cal thinks it's time for Abby to get a reality check, but how do you tell a mother that she should greet her child today because tomorrow may be too late. He just can't bring himself to tell her that there is no more hope. It's the term of your back against the wall. Sally's voice brings him back to the present. "Hi all, how are you?" She asked with concern in her eyes. Not waiting for an answer she walk to Jimmy's bed. What she sees before her, leaves her heart broken and she can not get a word out edgewise.

Cal turns to Abby and says: "Let's go get some coffee." Abby declaims the invitation, but Sally convinces her otherwise. "Abby I think you should go, take a break clear your head and I'll stay here with Jimmy in case he needs any thing." Abby agrees and leaves with Cal to get some coffee.

Sally sits on the edge of Jimmy's bed and looks at him trying her best to smile. "So how's the teddy bear? Have you thought of a name for him?" Jimmy opens his mouth to say something but Sally can see he is struggling and says: "Hush now, you can tell me the name you have chosen a bit later." There is a moment of silence when Sally asks: "Have you drawn your picture for Father Christmas to tell him what you want yet? Jimmy shakes his head, "I'll tell you what, Tell me what you want and I will write it down for you, Father Christmas knows that you are not feeling well so he will give you a free pass this year. If that's okay with you?" Jimmy looks at Sally for a moment, He nods his head in agreement. He opens his mouth and three vague words come out, Sally is not sure she heard right and repeats what he told her. He nodded his head to confirm that this is what he said. Sally walks towards the window. The tears roll down her cheeks. Her heart strings stirred at the thought of what he wants for Christmas. She pulled herself together then turned back to face Jimmy. She took a piece of paper from her purse again and wrote down Jimmy's wish. She then folds the paper and puts it back in her handbag. Sally looked at him and smiled.

Aunt Ella goes down on her knees as she had done every night. Since Jimmy was hospitalised she felt she should say a special prayer for him. Tonight she is praying for Abby. She puts her palms together, sighs and started to pray. "Lord the sigh that I gave now, consisted of all my worries. I read in the bible everyday of promises you make us. Lord you say that we must remind you of your promises. Tonight I stand before you reciting one of those promises. In Peter 5:7 you say Casting all your care upon him; for he careth for you. Lord, you helped me over come my pain and grief, and to make peace with your will. Please Lord Help Abby to accept your will. You know that death for her as a person, a bitter pill to swallow, and she has difficulty in bringing her heart into it. Lord You knows how she feels, and you know her heart's desire, for you have made her. Give her serenity in her heart, and clasping her in the hollow of your hand. Take all her worries and concerns, and turn her back to you. I take and place her before your feet, for you are the only one who can heal her. Take her pain away and fill with your glory and love. I ask this all of you Lord, not because I deserve it, but in your name only. Amen.

Chapter 13

Days go by and Jimmy condition worsens. All treatments have failed and there is no more hope for Jimmy. Everyone knows it but nobody dares saying it. Abby stays beside Jimmy day and night. Cal and Sally show there support by visiting each night. Aunt Ella has also come to visit a few times. Tonight everybody is there, Abby and Aunt Ella sit beside Jimmy and chat while Cal and Sally get some coffee. On the way to the cafeteria Sally says:" Abby told me that you took care of all of Jimmy's expenses." She hesitates but continues." She also told me that you proposed to her."

"I did. She didn't by any chance tell you what the answer is going to be?"

"No unfortunately she hasn't. You'll be the first to know. Don't pressure her to much, she is going through a rough time."

"I didn't intend to ask her now, but I couldn't postpone any longer. I am in love with her, I want to be her tower of strength. She needs to know that."

"You really are serious about her."

"Of course I'm serious about her, otherwise I would never have asked her to marry me."

"Yes that's true."

"Sally I get the feeling that you don't trust me. Is there something you want to get off your chest?" Sally bites her bottom lip and thinks about the conversation she and Abby had a week ago sitting by Jimmy's bedside. Sally had a feeling that there was more between them than just business. Abby confirmed her suspicions when she told Sally about the proposal. Sally was happy for Abby, that she finally found someone that loves her. After all the heartache and suffering she has endured in her life. She deserves to be happy and loved. Sally could see that something is bothering Abby, she didn't look like a women who had just said YES to the man she loved. She asked Abby what is bothering her, At first Abby wouldn't say, but Sally was determined and wouldn't let it go, she then decided to tell Sally.

Sally was suspicious of the accusations the blonde headed women made against Cal. She advised her that she should not believe everything she hears and should talk to Cal about it. Abby assured her that she paid no attention to the women's accusations at first, until she overheard a conversation between Cal and Leonie and began to wonder if the accusations were true. "Sally I can't marry a man that is willing to throw away his own flesh and blood so easily. His wife left him because he betrayed her. He will probably do the same to me, what makes me any different from the others?" Sally didn't have an answer for her. Since they had that conversations Sally has been having a strange feeling that she can't seem to shake. Something doesn't fit. But how can she argue with Abby about something that she heard with her own ears?

An impatient Cal makes her aware of him, He is waiting for an answer, Sally gets a hold of herself." I'm just very worried about her, I don't want her to get hurt. These past few months have been hell for her and now Jimmy . . . ."

"Why would I hurt Abby? I told you I'm in love with her, what could I possibly gain from hurting her anyway." Sally's facial expression shows Cal that she is doubting his intentions and Cal picks it up. "Sally. Why do I get the feeling that you are hiding something from me? If there is something you want to tell me, now is your chance." Sally knows there is no turning back now. Uncomfortably Sally speaks:" Fine I will tell you, but not here and not now. When visiting hours are over we can go have a drink someplace and I will tell you everything. Cal still doesn't look convinced, but what can do? Actually she is right, a hospital is no place for that kind of conversation. "Okay then, after visiting hours."

"We better get back to the others. They will start wondering what happened to us."

Jimmy falls asleep. Aunt Ella and Abby take a seat in the plastic chairs. There is a silence in the room. Both of the women engulfed in there own thoughts. She puts her head in her hands and let's out a great sigh as she thinks of Jimmy lying in the bed. Aunt Ella places her hand on Abby's shoulder and give her and encouraging squeeze. Abby lifts her head and stares into the open wall in front of her. Suddenly she starts talking. "Jimmy asked me if he was in heaven the other day. He says that my father once told him that in Heaven everyone is dressed in white clothing." The tears are running down Abby's face. "I wish he was here now." Aunt Ella asks: "Have you told Jimmy about his families death?" Abby stares at Aunt Ella with a sardonic look on her face. "There is nothing to tell. One of these days he will be at home and things will go back to normal. I don't want to upset him and cause a relapse in his condition." The silence follows for a while, Aunt Ella says: "Abby my dear, you must make peace with the will of God. I know that God's will is not always our will but know one thing my dear, God's will is the only will. He opens doors that no man can close and closes doors that no man can open."

Abby turns her head towards Aunt Ella: "How can you even say that? Do you not see the child lying on that bed? Look at him! What could he have possibly done to deserve this? Why must this happen to him? He is an innocent child." Cal and Sally are standing at the door but neither Abby or Aunt Ella notice them. "If God's will is the best why does he allow us to get hurt? How can God allow a three year olds body to devoured by a virus? No Aunt Ella." Abby gives a bitter laugh. "This time I have to disagree with you. God's will is not always the best for us.

Sally takes Aunt Ella home before meeting with Cal. She enters the bar and immediately notices him sitting at the counter. Cal becomes aware of Sally when she speaks to him. "Sorry if I kept you waiting, but I first wanted to make sure Aunt Ella was all right before I left." While Cal waited for Sally he ordered a drink. He asks her if she would also like one. "After what happened tonight, I think I need something really strong. Make it a single brandy on the rocks." Cal waves to the barmen and orders Sally's drink. He waits for her drink to arrive before he starts talking. "It must be very hard for Abby to acknowledge that Jimmy end is near."

"You can say that again, especially as she has just gone through it a few months ago. My heart bleeds for her." Sally takes a sip of her brandy and looks at Cal. Cal thinks about what Sally has just said. It's probably Jimmy dad that she is referring to. Even though he is dying to find out more about Jimmy's father, he rather not ask, after all there are more important things that he would like to know. "What is that you couldn't tell me at the medical centre?" Sally gets uncomfortable with the question, she knows she will have to tell him. She looks him straight in the eye and says: "Abby is not going to marry you. She is going to say no." Cal is outraged and can't get a word out. Sally sees it and says:

"I am sorry Cal. I didn't mean to say it so heartlessly, but that was her decision. She is going to tell you herself, I don't know when but at least you are prepared now." Cal came to his senses and asks: "May I at least know why she has decided not to marry me?" Sally feels sorry for him and decides to tell him the whole story. "Shortly after Abby started working for you she had a visit from a blonde headed women. I think her name was, um . . . . oh yes Lionie. She told Abby that you are a man that gets around between the women. That's why your wife left you. Abby didn't believe her at first but . . . ."

"But what Sally?"

"Abby didn't believe it at first. Until she was working late one night and overheard to people talking, she didn't mean to eavesdrop but the voices got loader and loader as she walked towards the elevator. She realised that it was your voice along with that other women. She immediately new it was your voice." Cal thinks back to the conversation he had with Lionie. She told him that she is pregnant. If Abby heard the conversation then why would she be upset? Sally sees the confused look on his face. She can't understand why he would be confused. "Can you not remember having a conversation with that women?"

"Of course I can remember the conversation, what I don't understand is if Abby heard the conversation, why would she refuse my proposal?"

Sally is staring at him with her mouth hanging open, she is so annoyed with Cal and says: "If I heard that a man can turn away his own flesh and blood then I would also turn down his proposal." She gets up as she walks away he grabs her by the arm. Sally swings around and looks up into dark grey eyes filled with rage. "What exactly do you mean by that?" Sally is now filled with anger. Sally gives him a cynical look. "Do you want me to spell it out for you? Abby has no interest in marrying you. First of all you're not a one woman man, secondly you use them, and when they fall pregnant you discard them along with your unborn child, then you move on to your next victim. Now do you understand why Abby doesn't want to marry you? Abby is terrified that you would do the same to her. Abby ha been trough a lot lately and she doesn't need you to complicate things further." With all the accusations sally has accused Cal with, angers him a lot. Cal grind's his teeth while saying: "You are barking up the wrong tree, Sally." From what you have told me now, it's obvious Abby didn't hear the whole conversation. Sit down and listen." Cal commands Sally and she feels intimidated and obeys. Cal informs Sally about the entire conversation him and Leonie. After his done Sally holds her head in shame and apologizes. "I'm sorry for jumping to conclusions . . . . But why don't you tell Abby this?"

"Now is not the time, she has got more important things to worry about."

Chapter 14

Abby must have fallen asleep and was suddenly woken up by someone shaking her gently. It's one of the nurses. The nurse speaks in a soft voice: "Ms Spence, the doctor would like to see you."

"Yes, of course."

"Follow me please."

Abby looked one last time at the sleeping child before she followed the nurse out the room. They go into a long hallway with rooms on both sides.

As they are walking she looked into every room. Some of the children lying in their beds. The others sat on their parents' laps. How she longed for the times that Jimmy would sit on her lap and she would hold him tightly against her heart. The times when they were together in the park playing, and even the nights that he kept her awake. Just to hold him in her arm one more time would mean the world to her. She can't though because his body get to sore.

The nurse comes to a holt and Abby had to put on the brakes otherwise she would have walked right into her. The nurse looked at her and Abby sees sympathy in the eyes: "Ms Spence, feel free to go inside and have a seat. The doctor will be with you shortly. Abby nods her head as she doesn't trust herself to speak. She went into the doctors office and takes a seat on a chair in front of the desk. She had barely sat down when someone closed the office door behind her. She turned around and saw a familiar face. The man before her looks surprised to see her and says: "Abby . . . . Spence?"

"Yes it's me."

"Jimmy Spence's guardian?"

"Yes, that's right." He took a seat in the chair opposite her.

"Do you recognise me?"

"Yes, I remember you. You are the man who broke my fall on my first day at Blake Attorneys. If I remember correctly you said your name was Mark." The man smiled. "Yes that's right Mark Bailey."

Suddenly he remembers why he had the nurse call her in. He looks down at his hands and up at her again." Abby this is very difficult for me to say to you, but I have to. We have tried all possible treatments to save Jimmy, but nothing is has worked, his condition worsens every day. As I'm sure you have noticed he can't even sit up straight anymore. I'm sorry but there is nothing more we can do for him, except make him comfortable and relieve him of as much pain as possible. Abby stares and him with tears rolling down her face. Without saying a word she gets up and walks out of the office. She walks back crying all the way to Jimmy's room. It's so hard for her to believe that that Jimmy isn't coming home again, now she will be all alone in the apartment. No, No! Shout's her insides. He will come home, don't worry about it. He must just get better. Abby walks back into Jimmy's room and sees that he is awake. She stands beside him and takes his hand like many times before. She looks down at him and see his eyes are filled with tears.

A tear drop rolls down his cheek. Abby must look away. If not she will burst into tears. She hears a child's voice talk to her: "Abby . . . . Come lywe by me pwease." She climbs on the bed and lies down next to him. She holds him tight and can't hold the tears back any longer. "I want you to always remember no matter what that I love you Jimmy, I love you unconditionally."

"I lowve you to Abby." And with that Jimmy gives his last breath. Abby hold the deceased child tight against her heart and realises what just happened. "Jimmy? Sweet heart? No!!!!! No. Wake up! Open your eyes!"

She jumps off the bed and runs out the room she runs straight into Cal. He looks down at her face and it's as if he knows what has just happened. He pulls her close against him. Abby is sobbing. She hits him against the chest and fights with him to let her go, but he just pulls her even closer. The nurses must have heard the commotion because they are coming down the hall way. The sight they are seeing in front of them is nothing new, they have seen it a thousand times before. One of the nurses go and call the doctor. Cal takes Abby into one of the empty rooms and closes the door behind them. Once Abby has calmed down he lets go slightly and looks her in the eyes. Never in his life had he seen such grief in someone's eyes before.

Cal takes the apartment keys from Abby and opens the front door. He follows her inside and closes the door behind them. Abby stands in the middle of the apartment and a feeling of emptiness overcomes her. She feels so alone. A toy lying on the floor draws her attention, she bends down to pick it up. It's Jimmy's dinosaur. She takes the toy and holds it tightly against her as if it was Jimmy that she was holding. Cal stands behind her putting his arms around her. "I'm terribly sorry my love." Everything gets too much for Abby and she pulls away from him to look him in the eye. "Sorry? What exactly is it that you are sorry for?" Abby's eyes are filled with despise for the man standing before her. Cal wants to say something but Abby doesn't give him a chance. "The only thing that you should be sorry about is your poor unborn child and his mother that you are willing to throw away like a bag of garbage. You walk away as if it has nothing to do with you, as if they never existed. How can you be such a coward and so cold. How do you live with yourself? How do you sleep at night?"

"It doesn't bother me, because . . . ." Abby stops him from saying another word.

"It doesn't bother you because you are exactly like your mother! You are angry at her for leaving you, but you do the same thing to your unborn child. Don't pass judgement on your mother because you are exactly like her. The past is repeating itself."

Cal is very hurt by what Abby has just said, but he doesn't show it. "Have you finished? Are you going to give me a chance to explain?"

"There is nothing to explain. I know what I heard. Oh and another thing, my answer is no, No I will not marry you, because you are a gigolo, and things like love, trust and responsibility don't exist in your world. I can't enter into a marriage without it.

Cal struggles to control himself.

He feels as if he could take her, and shake her until she takes it all back, every last word. There is no truth in what she has just said and he knows it. He takes a step forward towards her and Abby moves to the kitchen, he sees that she is trying to get away from him and he moves even closer to her. Abby shouts at him. "Go! Get out my house, go! I never want to see you again! Never!" Cal looks worried about the women standing in front of him. It's as if she changed overnight into someone that he doesn't know. She is completely beside herself. He is just as upset, but it won't help talking to her now, it's of no use. He actually doesn't even want to try. She has pushed him out of her life with all the nasty things that she has said to him. She used his secrets that he trusted her with against him and accused him of inhuman things.

He turn and walks out the door, out of her life for now and forever. Abby curls herself into a ball on the kitchen floor.

For the second time in her life, not even far apart that she had to face the cruel death of a loved one.

Sally keeps herself busy during the past few days by planning Jimmy's funeral. She and Aunt Ella decided to handle the funeral, seeing as neither one of them could get in touch with Abby. Sally has tried on numerous occasions to phone Abby but she is not answering her telephone.

Aunt Ella has knocked on her apartment door a few times but no one opens the door. They are both very worried about Abby.

A week ago Sally arrive one afternoon for visiting hours and when she got to Jimmy's room she found an empty bed, she immediately enquired about it.

The nurse on duty informed her of what had happened. She could not utter a word. Turned around and walked. The nurse stopped her and asked what should be done with the big teddy bear still in the room. She told the nurse that she would take it with her. She placed the teddy bear in the spare room at her house. She opened a cupboard and took out her needle work box. She takes the unpicker out of the box and starts unpicking the hart that is on the teddy bear chest.

She took the letter that Jimmy had written to Father Christmas, slid it underneath the heart and sewed it back onto the teddy bear again. She turned as she was walking out the door and says with tears in her eyes: "I am going to miss you so much my Cheeky Chop." She left the room and closed the door softly behind her. She then got into her car and drove to Abby. Standing in front of Abby's apartment waiting for someone to open but no one does, she then decides to go to Aunt Ella to see if Abby may be with her. When Aunt Ella opened the door and Sally asked for Abby, Aunt Ella, assured her that she was not with her. Sally immediately called Cal at the office and he told her that the last time he saw her was the night of Jimmy's death and what happened between them. He also informed her that what happened between Abby and himself was something of the past and put down the telephone.

Aunt Ella was now very worried and questionably stared at Sally. Sally then told her what Cal had said.

"Oh no, Sally what should we do now?"

"I don't know Aunt Ella, We will have to make sure that Abby is okay." Again they walked to Abby's apartment and knocked on the door but still no one answered. Aunt Ella remembered that she had Abby's spare keys, In case of emergency.

She immediately when to get the keys and they unlocked Abby's apartment door. Hastily they entered the apartment only to find Abby lying in Jimmy's bed fast asleep. They left quietly and returned to Aunt Ella's apartment. Aunt Ella put the kettle on and made then some tea. It's then when Sally says: "Aunt Ella, what are we going to do about the funeral? I doubt that Abby will do it. I will have to do it on her behalf."

"I agree Sally, I don't think that Abby is of right mind to make any arrangements."

Sally went directly from Aunt Ella to the funeral parlour. She began the arrangements. They agreed on a cremation. When Sally left the funeral parlour all of the important arrangements had been made. The only thing left to do was to get a pastor for the ceremony. That task she left to Aunt Ella.

Abby awakes with a child's voice calling her name. She sits up straight in the bed looking for Jimmy. Then it hits her, Jimmy isn't here anymore and will never be again. She is completely alone and there is a darkness and emptiness that fills her inside. She falls back onto the pillow and closes her eyes. Suddenly she remembers Aunt Ella's words. "If God brings you to the edge of a cliff you have to let go and fully trust in him. If you fall one of two things will happen. He will either catch you or teach you how to fly."

The words play over and over in her head. No matter how hard she tries she can't seem to get it out of her head. Abby gets up to make herself a cup of tea. As she makes her way to the kitchen she notices a white piece of paper laying at the front door.

She walks closer and picks it up. Someone must have slid it under the door. She looks at it and sees her name written on it. She opens the letter and her stomach starts turning as she reads the it. It's a letter from Sally sharing with her that Jimmy's funeral will be held the next day. She provided Abby with the time and place as well. Abby feels the tears running down her cheeks, she crumples up the paper and throws it across the room. She takes a seat on one of the couches and pulls her knees under her. She sits like that for a while and thinks about Sally's note. Longing fills her once again as she thinks of her parents, her sister and Jimmy that were taken away from her in such a short period of time. She is angry and heartbroken. Why must she go through all this pain? Aunt Ella said that God's will is the best thing for us as people, but why is God's will so cruel? Why does it feel like God has turned his back on her? Why does his hand feel so far away from her? Aunt Ella said, The Lord will never forsake us nor will he leave us. But today Abby feels very much alone.

Chapter 15

After Sally put the envelope under Abby's door, she gets in her car and drove off to Blake, Attorneys. While she is driving she thinks to herself. Oh I hope Cal is at the office and available. She has been trying to get hold of him, but he doesn't answer his phone and she have left like a dozen messages. Today she decided to take the bull by the horn and go to him.

At the big old grey building, Sally parks her car, and get out. She enters the building and walk towards the reception area. "Good morning my name is Sally Coater, and I need to see Mr Cal Blake." Irene looks at her and ask: "Do you have an appointment Miss Coater?"

"No, but it is relatively urgent. If you could maybe just call him and tell him I am here . . . ."

"I'm sorry Miss Coater. Mr Blake only see people by appointments."

"But I need to see him now!"

"Sally what's all the fuss about?" Sally turns around only to see Cal standing behind her. She takes a deep breath and say: "Cal I would like to speak to you. It will only take a minute of your time."

"I'm actually on my way to a meeting."

"Please Cal, like I said it will only take a minute of your time." Cal sees the supplication in Sally's eyes and says: "Fine then, I listen to what you have to say."

"Thank you Cal it's well appreciated."

"Come this way." Sally follows Cal trough a door that leads into a large room. This must be the board room, because of the long table and many chairs that surrounds it. Sally decides. Cal closes the door behind him and takes a seat on one of the chairs.

Sally takes at seat next to him. She opens her purse and hands him a envelope. Cal takes it from her and opens it. He empties the envelope, unfold the paper and begins to read it. When finished reading the letter, he looks at Sally. She moves uncomfortably in her chair.

"I thought you might want to know about the funeral that takes place tomorrow afternoon. Even though you didn't know him that well . . . . What you had done for him the last few days, was noble. Cal sees the tears rolling down Sally's cheeks and say: "He must have been a really special little boy."

"Oh he was my Cheeky-chop. I'm going to miss him a lot. I can still recall the day when I went to visit Abby. The door was unlock and so I went in her apartment.

I called her and she answered that she was in the bedroom. So I went straight to the bedroom, and there I discovered Abby rearranging her bedroom with a little boy standing in a corner, holding only one bag in his hand. He looked so lost and scared. I was very confused. I didn't know what was going on.

So later that evening after everything was in place, I ordered us some pizza. After we've eaten, I helped Abby clean up and then I asked her about the boy. She had a devastated look in her eyes and the only thing she said was he came for a visit. It was clear that the subject was not open for discussion. I left early that evening but didn't go home. I parked my car around the corner and went to see aunt Ella. At first she said it's Abby business and we shouldn't interfere, but somehow I convinced Aunt Ella to tell me.

My hart bled for Abby when I heard what had happened. Abby's parents, sister and Cheeky-chop were on they way from Beaufort-West to visit her when it happened. Just before they reached Bloemfontein they had a head on collision with a truck. Apparently the truck driver fell asleep, went over into the oncoming traffic and hit them. Both Abby's parents and sister died on impact. Little Jimmy was the only survivor with not even a scratch on him. What's so ironic, is six months later he dies of a virus. I can't stop wondering, what was the purpose?

Anyway, ever since the accident, Jimmy stayed with Abby. I honestly don't know how Abby is going to make it this time. Apparently she never accepted her families death. Jimmy was her only hope that they will arrive someday. She didn't even attend their funeral, and I'm afraid she won't attend Jimmy's either. Abby can't accept death nor can she deal with it.

That's why Aunt Ella and I took the responsibility of the arrangements of Jimmy's funeral on our shoulders." Sally looks at Cal and sees the total confusion on his face. "What's wrong? Did I say something . . ."

"No, no . . . . It's not something you said . . . . All this time I thought Jimmy was Abby's son. They look so much alike."

"It's probably because Abby and her sister were identical twins."

"The other night when you mentioned not long ago she also lost someone very close to her. I thought you were referring to Jimmy's Father." Sally looks very surprised. "Oh no . . . Jimmy was Abby's sister's son, and his father . . . . Well I don't know were he is, or what happened to him, but one things for sure, he abandoned that little boy and his mother."

Everything falls into place. Now Cal can understand why Abby were so hard on him. She is hurt and there are so many sorrows that she have to bare. All of this she is facing on her own with no shoulder to lean on and no one to support her. Sally and Aunt Ella will always be there for her, but he doubt if it will be enough.

Cal closes his eyes, rest his head in his palms and thinks to himself. Is my love for her so unconditional that I can overcame the trust she broke?

It's a small funeral consisting of Aunt Ella, Sally, Doctor Grey, Doctor Bailey and a few nurses who spent Jimmy's last few days with him. Sally scans the room for Cal, but he is no where to be found. Just before the service begins, Cal moves in next to Sally. Her eyes thank him for the afford he made to come. The Pastor opens the ceremony with a prayer. Once he has said the prayer Abby walks in and takes a seat right at the back of the church. The Pastor begins preaching.

"Today I read from Ecclesiastes 3:1 and 2. *"To every thing there is a reason, and a time. To every purpose under heaven: A time to be born, and a time to die; a time to plant, and a time to pluck up that which is planted."*

He closes his bible and looks down at the people sitting beneath him. "Brothers and sisters, someone once said. As the years are divided into seasons, so are man's life also divided into seasons. Everything that happens in life, can be compared to a season we go trough.

The season we come to stand before today, is the season of pain and sorrow, because we must say goodbye to a loved one. Times like these we usually want the season to chance, so we can once again experience the seasons of happiness. Times like these, we are inclined to depend on our own strength to process our hurt, but it's not what God wants us to do.

The Lord wants us to depend on his strength to process our hurt. God's strength is a solid anchor when it feels to us as man like the spring will never dawn. God's power comes in times when we feel we are on our worst and when the storms of live won't seem to calm. The season of death, is the one season we always want to avoid. We don't want to say good bye and sometimes, God takes us trough this season to teach us how to say good bye.

God will continue to take us trough the same season over and over until we've learned to depend on His strength and until we learned to accept His best will. Sometimes He works trough people to help us, sometimes it's necessary for Him to take us aside and teach us separately. It's time for us as man to comprehend that God rule and govern our minute lives.

When will we realize, in times like these when it feels like our wailing won't subside, the only place where we can find rest and peace, is at Jesus' feet."

In Romans 5 God says: "*You see, at just the right time, when we were still powerless, Christ died for the ungodly. Since we have been justified by his blood, how much more shall we be saved from God's wrath through him. For if, when we were God's enemies, we were reconciled to him through the death of his Son, how much more, having been reconciled, shall we be saved through his life. Not only is this so, but we also rejoice in God through our Lord Jesus Christ, through whom we have now received reconciliation.*"

Abby closes her eyes, and for the first time since the accident she speaks to the Lord in her mind.

"Lord please forgive me for not accepting your will and for thinking that I don't need you in my life. The past six months I felt so lonely, but I know it was me that moved away from You and not the other way around. I want to come back to You and declare my love. Today I've realized how vain I am before You. Lord please teach me how to be humble again, and please me help to conquer my grief."

Abby opens her eyes which are filled with tears, only to hear the last part of the preach.

"Let's take God's hand and allow him to lead us trough the seasons of life."

Later that afternoon Sally knocks on Abby's apartment door. Abby opens the door and is happy to see her best friend. She then invites her inside and closes the door behind Sally. Sally takes place on one of the couches and the packed suitcase caught her eye. "And this? Are you leaving?"

"Relax Sally. I am going somewhere, but I am coming back. It's time for me to take a journey trough my past, so that I can start my future. I need to go back and burn my bridges."

"Does this means . . . . ? Are you finally . . . . ?" Sally can't say anything else because she burst into tears. Abby takes a seat next to her and says: "I want to go to their grave . . . . to say . . . . goodbye. I'm taking Jimmy's ashes with me to put it beside his mothers grave."

"Oh Abby. I'm so glad for you. It's going to be hard, but I'm here for you every step of the way."

Yesterday when Abby arrived in Beauford-West, she drove trough the streets of her hometown. She stopped the car in front of the house which her parents rented since as long as she can remember.

She looked at the house and memories of her childhood doomed up before her. She remembered how she and Cathy use to play on the lawn. Their mother would normally sit on the porch and watch over them. The garden that once was her mothers pride, is now very neglected. Her parents were the last residents of the house. The old couple which has been their neighbours for years, informed her that the house has been sold.

Aunt Beth and Uncle Sam were so happy to see her again. They ask her were she is staying at, and she named a guest house. They said they won't allow her to stay in a guest house, she must come and stay with them. They would not take no for an answer so Abby gave in and stayed the night. That night at the dinner table aunt Beth told Abby were her family was buried. This morning she packed up all of her belongings and said goodbye to the elderly couple. She got in the car and drove towards the graveyard.

With tears in her eyes, Abby is standing before the graves of her family. She bends down and puts a little box that contains Jimmy's ashes on top of her sisters grave.

"Cathy I thank you for the little time you borrowed him to me. I now know why you always referred to him as your angel. His is indeed a angel. I'm sorry I never told him about your death. I deliberately kept it away from him, because I didn't want to talk about it. It hurt to much even when I thought about it. I couldn't accept that you're gone, and not coming back. I love you Cathy, and rest in peace." Abby stoke the box with Jimmy's ashes in it.

"Jimmy, I'm sorry I was so trapped in my own grief that I forgot that you have also lost what I did. I'm going to miss you. I love you lots, and now you really are in heaven and I know that you have no more pain. Mom, dad, I'm sorry it took me so long to come to your grave. I've made peace with your death and with God's will. I know that God has a plan with my life, but what his plan is, I will just have to wait and see. I love you both, and hope to see you one day"

Abby turns around with tears flowing down her cheeks. It feels to her like someone has just lift a mountain off her shoulders. She walks towards Sally's car, but is not aware of the man that is waiting there for her. The only thing she can think about now is Aunt Ella's words, and she knows, God taught her how to fly . . . .

Abby looks up only to see Cal standing at Sally's car. "What are you doing here?"

"I came to get my wife to be."

"Cal please I can't marry you."

"Why not"

"Cal you know why not."

"Because you think I'm responsible for Leonie's pregnancy, and I've abandon her and my unborn child?"

"Please Cal now is not the time for this. I need to go now. If still got a long way to drive."

"Abby all I ask you is just to hear me out." Cal looks at Abby and she can see the supplication in his eyes. "Fine but please make it quick."

"The conversation that you heard between Leonie and myself . . . . Is not what you think. You only heard a quarter of what was said between us. Leonie is pregnant but not because of me. She and my best friend, Mark Bailey were married once, but they got divorced because she deceived him. He caught her with another man in bed. She came to plead with me to talk to Mark, because she knew he would listen to me. She only then told me she was pregnant. At first I told her she is on her own. I knew how Mark felt because it happened to me as well. The pregnancy got stuck in my mind so I spoke to Mark and he did consider marrying her again, but then he discovered it's not his baby.

Abby . . . . maybe this will change how you feel about me, maybe it won't. I just wanted to tell you this, because you see . . . . I've done some real soul searching and I really do love you. Even thought you never said you love me and don't want to marry me, I couldn't bare the thought of you hating me." Then he turns around and start walking until Abby's words makes him pause in his footsteps. "Cal wait . . . . I am sorry for all the awful things I said to you. You trusted me with your deepest secret and used it against you. It's not that I don't love you, because I do love you and it's not that I don't want to marry you, I really do." He turns around and start walking back to her. "Then what is holding you back Abby?"

"A marriage can't be build without trust and you don't trust me. That's what you told Sally."

"During my soul searching I also realized that love conquers all. I came to understand the situation you were in. I wouldn't have done the exact same thing, but I understand and I forgive you."

"Oh Cal what have I done to deserve you?"

"I was thinking the same thing, luckily we have the rest of our lives to figure that out together." Before Call could kiss her she pulls away. "What's wrong my love is there another mountain I need to move?"

"Actually there is." Cal looks at Abby and frown. "What might that mountain be?"

"Flippie and his family."

Epilogue

It's a wonderful summers morning. Aunt Ella is working in the garden and little Jimmy is helping her. Aunt Ella makes the wholes in the ground and carefully places the Dahlia bulbs into the wholes which she then covers with soil. Jimmy keeps himself busy by pulling out the weeds here and there.

Abby and Cal whom have been married now for four very happy years, are sitting hand in hand on the back porch watching their beautiful son. It has become a ritual for Aunt Ella, Sally and Mark to come visit for Christmas. As usual Sally and Mark are late. Abby turns to Cal and says: "I wonder when Sally and Mark will arrive?" Her words are barely spoken when the front door bell rings. Cal gets up. "It's probably them now."

"I hope so."

Cal disappears into the house and a few moments later he returns with Sally and Mark right behind him.

"Hey Abbs."

"Oh, Hi Sally." They hug each other. She turns to greet Mark and sees what he holds in his hand. She looks at Sally and asks:" Why does this teddy bear look so familiar?"

"It's the teddy bear I gave to Jimmy when he was in the medical centre."

"Where did you find it?"

"While I was clearing the house, I happened to come across it in the attic. I thought you might want to have it for Jimmy?" She smiles, takes the big furry bear from Mark and calls Jimmy over. "Jimmy come look at what Aunt Sally brought for you." Jimmy and Aunt Ella come to the porch. Jimmy can't believe his eyes. He has never seen such a big teddy bear in his life. "Wow, thanko, Aunty Sal." He holds the bear tight. "It's my please big boy, but remember you must look after him. He belonged to a very special young boy and his name was also Jimmy." Jimmy nods his head. "I will I pwomise." He turn to show Aunt Ella his new toy. With a frown on Abby's face she turns and asks Sally: "Did I hear you correctly, you said you were clearing out your house?" Sally and Mark giggle. Abby and Cal see something is going on between the two of them. Sally can't keep it to herself anymore and she blurted it out: "We are getting married in two months."

"What, when did this happen?" Abby and Cal are both equally surprised. "Mark ask me a while ago."

"Why didn't you say anything?" Mark interrupts. "Don't ask, it's a long story, You know your husband wasn't the only one with women troubles. I struggled just as much to convince Sally. She finally gave in and said yes." Sally nudges him in the ribs. "Oh please, you didn't suffer as much as Cal did." Mark puts his hand on his heart as if Sally just hurt his feelings. They all burst out in laughter.

"We are very happy for you two. Remember all good things come to those who wait. Look how long my wife waited for me." It's Abby's turn to nudge Cal in the ribs. "Your so funny Cal." They all laugh together.

After lunch Abby, Sally and Aunt Ella sit on the porch chatting. Cal took Mark to show him his new sports car. Jimmy and his new best friend, teddy bear are playing on the lawn. He makes the teddy bear lie down next to him and rolls over it. While he rolls over it he pulls it along with him. He rolls once again and his finger gets stuck between the heart on the teddy bears chest and the actual teddy bear. The next moment he is sitting with the heart in his hand. Aunt Sally told him to take special care of his teddy bear, and he bursts into tears because he broke it. "Oh no!" Suddenly he stops crying he sees a piece of paper lying on the grass next to the teddy bear. He picks it up and hands it to his mother. "Mommy wook hewe."

"What is this? Where did you find it?"

"It did fawl out of my teddy beawr." He points toward the teddy bear lying on it's back on the grass, with the piece of material lying next to it. Abby frowns and unfolds the piece of paper. Just the hand writing tells her it belongs to Sally. "I think this belongs to you." Abby hands the note to Sally. She reads the note, and somewhere in the back of her mind it rings a bell. "I know it's my hand writing, but it doesn't belong to me. It belongs to my Cheeky Chop Jimmy." Now Sally has got every ones attention, she continues. "Jimmy asked me to write a note to Father Christmas before he died, telling him what he would like for Christmas." Sally pauses to gather her emotions, she continues. "Actually if I think about it, Jimmy did get his Christmas wish after all, he wished to see his family again, his mother and grandparents . . . . and so he did."

CPSIA information can be obtained
at www.ICGtesting.com
Printed in the USA
BVOW08s1203260318
511604BV00002B/253/P